FEE FI FO FUM

He was big, this giant. Bigger than any creature Jacky had ever seen. His head alone was more than two feet high, almost a foot and a half wide. Legs, three yards long, supported the enormous bulk of his torso and carried him across the park. He was going to be right on top of her in moments and she didn't know what to do. She was too petrified with fear to do more than shake where she was crouched. Her fingers plucked nervously at the hem of her jacket and she chewed furiously on her lower lip.

Run, she told herself. Get up and run, you fool.

JACK, THE GIANT-KILLER

CHARLES DE LINT

ACE BOOKS, NEW YORK

This Ace Book contains the complete text of the original hardcover edition. It has been completely reset in a typeface designed for easy reading, and was printed from new film.

JACK, THE GIANT-KILLER
THE JACK OF KINROWAN:
A NOVEL OF URBAN FAERIE

An Ace Book/published by arrangement with
The Endicott Studio

The Fairy Tales series is produced by
Terri Windling, Endicott Studio,
63 Endicott Street, Boston, Massachusetts 02113.

PRINTING HISTORY
Ace hardcover edition/November 1987
Ace mass-market edition/January 1990

ISBN: 0-441-37970-2

Ace Books are published by The Berkley Publishing Group,
200 Madison Avenue, New York, New York 10016.
The name "ACE" and the "A" logo are trademarks
belonging to Charter Communications, Inc.

PRINTED IN THE UNITED STATES OF AMERICA

10 9 8 7 6 5 4 3 2 1

for

MaryAnn and Terri

and dedicated
to the memory of
K.M. Briggs
(1898–1980)

Red is the colour of magic in every country,
and has been so from the very earliest times.
The caps of fairies and musicians are well-
nigh always red.

> —W.B. Yeats,
> from *Fairy and Folk Tales
> of the Irish Peasantry*

Rowan am I and I   am sister to the Red Man
my berries are guarded   by dreamless dragons
my wood charms the   spells from witches
and in the wide plain   my floods quicken

> —Wendlessen,
> from *The Calendar of the Trees*

Though she be but little, she is fierce.

> —William Shakespeare,
> from *A Midsummer-Night's Dream*

INTRODUCTION
FAIRY TALES

There is no satisfactory equivalent to the German word *märchen*, tales of magic and wonder such as those collected by the Brothers Grimm: *Rapunzel*, *Hansel & Gretel*, *Rumpelstiltskin*, *The Six Swans* and other such familiar stories. We call them fairy tales, although none of the above stories actually contains a creature called a "fairy." They do contain those ingredients most familiar to us in fairy tales: magic and enchantment, spells and curses, witches and trolls, and protagonists who defeat overwhelming odds to triumph over evil. J.R.R. Tolkien, in his classic essay on Fairy Stories, offers the definition that these are not in particular tales about fairies or elves, but rather of the land of Faerie: "the Perilous Realm itself, and the air that blows in the country. I will not attempt to define that directly," he goes on, "for it cannot be done. Faerie cannot be caught in a net of words; for it is one of its qualities to be indescribable, though not imperceptible."

Fairy tales were originally created for an adult audience. The tales collected in the German countryside and set to paper by the Brothers Grimm (wherein a Queen orders her stepdaughter, Snow White, killed and her heart served "boiled and salted for my dinner" and a peasant girl must cut off her own feet lest the Red Shoes, of which she has been so vain, keep her dancing night and day until she dances herself to death) were published for an adult readership, popular, in the age of Göethe and Schiller, among the German Romantic poets. Charles Perrault's spare and moralistic tales (such as Little Red Riding Hood who, in the original Perrault telling, gets eaten by the wolf in the end for having the ill sense to talk to strangers in the wood) was written for the court of Louis XIV; Madame d'Aulnoy (author of *The White Cat*) and Madam Leprince de Beaumont (author of *Beauty and the Beast*) also wrote for the French aristocracy. In England, fairy stories and heroic legends were popularized through Malory's Arthur, Shakespeare's Puck and Ariel, Spencer's Faerie Queen.

With the Age of Enlightenment and the growing emphasis on rational and scientific modes of thought, along with the rise in fashion of novels of social realism in the Nineteenth Century, literary fantasy went out of vogue and those stories of magic, enchantment, heroic quests and courtly romance that form a cultural heritage thousands of years old, dating back to the oldest written epics and further still to tales spoken around the hearth-fire, came to be seen as fit only for children, relegated to the nursery like, Professor Tolkien points out, "shabby or old-fashioned furniture . . . primarily because the adults do not want it, and do not mind if it is misused."

And misused the stories have been, in some cases altered so greatly to make them suitable for Victorian children that the original tales were all but forgotten. Andrew Lang's *Tam Lin*, printed in the colored Fairy Books series, tells the story of little Janet whose playmate is stolen away by the fairy folk—ignoring the original, darker tale of seduction and human sacrifice to the Lord of Hell, as the heroine, pregnant with Tam Lin's child, battles the Fairy Queen for her lover's life. Walt Disney's "Sleeping Beauty" bears only a little resemblance to Straparola's *Sleeping Beauty of the Wood*, published in Venice in the Sixteenth Century, in which the enchanted princess is impregnated as she sleeps. The Little Golden Book version of the *Arabian Nights* resembles not at all the violent and sensual tales recounted by Scheherazade in *One Thousand and One Nights* so that the King of Kings won't take her virginity and her life.

* * *

The wealth of material from myth and folklore at the disposal of the story-teller (or modern fantasy novelist) has been described as a giant cauldron of soup into which each generation throws new bits of fancy and history, new imaginings, new ideas, to simmer along with the old. The story-teller is the cook who serves up the common ingredients in his or her own individual way, to suit the tastes of a new audience. Each generation has its cooks, its Hans Christian Andersen or Charles Perrault, spinning magical tales for those who will listen—even amid the Industrial Revolution of the Nineteenth Century or the technological revolution of our own. In the last century, George MacDonald, William Morris, Christina Rossetti, and Oscar Wilde, among others, turned their hands to fairy stories; at the turn of the century lavish fairy tale collections were produced, a showcase for the art of Arthur Rackham, Edmund Dulac, Kay Nielson, the Robinson Brothers—published as children's books, yet often found gracing adult salons.

In the early part of the Twentieth Century Lord Dunsany, G.K. Chesterton, C.S. Lewis, T.H. White, J.R.R. Tolkien—to name but a few—created classic tales of fantasy; while more recently we've seen the growing popularity of books published under the category title "Adult Fantasy"—as well as works published in the literary mainstream that could easily go under that heading: John Barth's *Chimera*, John Gardner's *Grendel*, Joyce Carol Oates' *Bellefleur*, Sylvia Townsend Warner's *Kingdoms of Elfin*, Mark Halprin's *A Winter's Tale*, and the works of South American writers such as Gabriel García Márquez and Miguel Angel Asturias.

It is not surprising that modern readers or writers should occasionally turn to fairy tales. The fantasy story or novel differs from novels of social realism in that it is free to portray the world in bright, primary colors, a dream-world half remembered from the stories of childhood when all the world was bright and strange, a fiction unembarrassed to tackle the large themes of Good and Evil, Honor and Betrayal, Love and Hate. Susan Cooper, who won the Newbery Medal for her fantasy novel *The Grey King*, makes this comment about the desire to write fantasy: "In the 'Poetics' Aristotle said, 'A likely impossibility is always preferable to an unconvincing possibility.' I think those of us who write fantasy are dedicated to making impossible things seem likely, making dreams seem real. We are somewhere between the Impressionist and abstract painters. Our writing is haunted by those parts of our experience which we do not understand, or even consciously remember. And if you, child or adult, are drawn to our work, your response comes from that same shadowy land.''

All Adult Fantasy stories draw in a greater or lesser degree from traditional tales and legends. Some writers consciously acknowledge that material, such as J.R.R. Tolkien's use of themes and imagery from the Icelandic Eddas and the German Niebelungenlied in *The Lord of the Rings* or Evangeline Walton's reworking of the stories from the Welsh Mabinogion in *The Island of the Mighty*. Some authors use the language and symbols of old tales to create new ones, such as the stories collected in Jane Yolen's *Tales of Wonder*, or Patricia McKillip's *The Forgotten Beasts of Eld*. And others, like Robin McKinley in *Beauty* or Angela Carter in *The Bloody Chamber* (and the movie ''The Company of Wolves'' derived from a story in that collection) base their stories directly on old tales, breathing new life into them, and presenting them to the modern reader.

The Fairy Tales series presents new novels of the later sort—novels directly based on traditional fairy tales. Each novel in the series is firmly based on a specific, often familiar, tale—yet each author is free to use that tale as he or she pleases, showing the diverse ways a modern story-teller can approach traditional material.

The novel you hold in your hands brings the old tales of *Jack the Giant-Killer* and *Jack and the Beanstalk*, as well as other bits of fairy lore, to modern day Canada—by an author who has gained a wide following for his ability to weave mythic motifs with modern characterizations and settings, creating Fairy Tales for the Twentieth Century. Other novels in the Fairy Tales series include a romantic retelling of *Rose White, Rose Red*; Hans Christian Andersen's *The Nightingale* as a Japanese historical fantasy; a reworking of the Hungarian *The Sun, the Moon, and the Stars* into a thought-provoking modern novel; a moody and beautiful retelling of *The Briar*

Rose . . . and much more. Fantasy and horror by some of the most talented writers in these two fields, retelling the world's most beloved tales, in editions lovingly designed—as all good Fairy Tale books should be. We hope you'll enjoy them.

FOREWORD

All characters and events in this book are fictitious and any resemblance to actual persons living or dead is purely coincidental.

It was in the late summer of 1984 that Terri Windling first told me of her concept for a series of novel-length retellings of traditional fairy tales and asked me if I'd be interested in doing one. The idea was so intriguing—especially when she mentioned that said stories could take place in any setting—that without waiting for a contract, or even to find out if she could place the series, I immediately sat down to work on my contribution to it.

The principal reason for my interest was that I'd been wanting to write a high fantasy placed in a contemporary setting for some time. I liked the novels that I'd written to date using this general concept, but I felt that the actual blending of faerie with an urban setting had worked with only varying degrees of success. In them, faerie was still an intrusion into the real world, rather than something that was always present, but invisible to the casual glance. This fairy tale series of Terri's seemed the perfect opportunity to try to get it right.

My first inclination was to pick an obscure fairy tale to work with but, as I reread those old stories, I kept coming back to the trickster figure of Jack—the Jack of "Jack and the Beanstalk," "Jack the Giant-Killer," or the Wee Jack stories of Scottish folklore. Jack wins out as much by luck as by pluck; Jack's both foolish and clever. And enamoured as I am with the role of the trickster in all his guises, I soon realized that I had no choice: It had to be a Jack tale. The creative process being what it is, the words came to paper as soon as I settled on ''Jack the Giant-Killer'' as the principal framework for *The Jack of Kinrowan*.

As the novel grew, other tales and bits of folklore kept adding themselves to the brew. And so you'll find traces of ''Kate Crackernuts'' in here, elements of the seven brothers who became swans, the youngest son of three who sets off to make his fortune, and all sorts of traditional folkloric material, from Billy Blinds to the restless dead of the Scottish Highlands.

I owe a great debt to Terri Windling, not only for sparking this particular story in my mind, but for her friendship and astute editing over the years. My wife MaryAnn also plays a major role in my creative processes, serving as the most discerning and beneficial of first readers. (And I used to just think that I was lucky that she married me.) My friend Rodger Turner has also provided valuable feedback on works in progress on an ongoing basis and I'd like to thank him here as well.

The source material for this novel of Urban Faerie has its roots in a lifetime of reading folk and fairy tales, and from years of listening to and playing traditional music. Some specific sources would include: K.M. Briggs, author of studies such as *The Anatomy of Puck*, *A Dictionary of Fairies*, and a couple of outstanding novels, of which I'd particularly recommend *Hobberdy Dick*; Alan Garner, known better for his Young Adult fantasies perhaps, but also a fine collector and reteller of traditional English fairy tales; and Jane Yolen, who over the years has produced a body of beautiful fairy tales that rivals any of the masters. The gruagaghs I got from Robin Williamson, one of the few surviving bards still practising his craft.

For those of you who are interested in more Urban Faerie stories, I currently have a second novel in draft form entitled *Drink Down the Moon*, a loose retelling of ''The Ogre, or Devil's Heart in the Egg.'' This one centers more on the fiaina sidhe, the solitary faerie briefly mentioned in *The Jack of Kinrowan*, and deals primarily with one Jemi Pook, a faerie sax player in an r&b band. Perhaps we'll meet again in its pages.

—Charles de Lint
Ottawa, winter 1987

JACK, THE
GIANT-KILLER

CHAPTER
1

The reflection that looked back at her from the mirror wasn't her own. Its hair was cut short and ragged like the stubble in a cornfield. Its eye make-up was smudged and the eyes themselves were red-veined and puffy. She hadn't been crying, but oh, she'd been drinking. . . .

"Jacky," she mumbled to the reflection. "What've you done to yourself this time?"

Five hours ago she'd numbly watched the door of her apartment slam shut behind Will.

"You're so goddamn predictable!" he'd shouted at the end. "Nothing changes the routine. It's just night after night of burrowing away in this place. What do I have to do to drag you away from your books or that glass tit? This place is a prison, Jacky, and I'm not buying into it. Not anymore. I'm tired of going out on my own, tired of . . . Christ, we've got absolutely nothing in common and I don't know what I ever thought we *did* have."

He'd stood there, red-faced, a vein throbbing at his temple, then turned and walked out the door. She knew he wasn't coming back. And after that outburst, she didn't *want* him back.

There was nothing wrong with being a homebody. There was nothing wrong with not wanting—not *needing*—the constant jostle and noise of a party or a bar or . . . whatever. Maybe it was better this way. She didn't need what Will offered any more than he seemed to want what she had. So why did she feel guilty? Why did she feel so . . . empty? Like there was something missing.

She remembered going to the window, reaching it in time to see Will disappearing down the street. Then she'd gone into the bathroom and stood in front of the mirror looking at herself. What was missing? Could you see it by just looking at her?

Her waist-length blonde hair hadn't been cut in twelve years—not since she was, God, seven. She was wearing her favorite clothes: a baggy plaid shirt and a comfortable pair of old Levi's. When she walked down the street, did people turn to look at her and maybe . . . laugh? Did they think she was some kind of hippie burn-out, even though she'd barely been out of diapers during the sixties?

She wasn't sure what had started it, but one moment she was just standing there in front of the mirror, and the next she had a pair of scissors in her hand and the long blonde tresses were falling to the floor, one after another, while she stood there saying, "I'm not empty inside," over and over trying to find some meaning in what she was doing. And when she was finished, she was more numb than when Will had walked out the door. There was a stranger staring at her out of the mirror.

She remembered fumbling with her make-up, smudging it as she put it on, smearing it some more as she knuckled her eyes. Finally she bolted from the apartment herself.

The October air was cooling as it got dark. The streets of Ottawa were slick from the rain that had been washing them for the better part of the afternoon. She walked aimlessly, stunned at what she had done, at how light her head felt, at the touch of the wind on her scalp.

She had gone into a bar and had a drink. Then had another. Then lost count. And now she was here, in some grimy bathroom, the sound of the bar's sound system booming through the ceiling from upstairs, some strange-looking punk-rocker staring back at her from the mirror, and she was too lost to do anything.

"Get out of here," she told her reflection. "Go home."

The door opened behind her and she started guiltily as a pair of young women entered the washroom. They were sleek, like *Vogue* models. Styled hair, high heels. They regarded her curiously, and Jacky fled their amused scrutiny, the washroom, the bar, and found herself on the streets, stumbling, because she was far from sober; cold, because she'd forgotten to bring a jacket; and empty . . . so empty inside.

She took Bank Street south from downtown, leaving behind the unhappy mix of old-fashioned stone buildings and new glass-and-steel office complexes that looked more like men's cologne containers when she walked under the Queensway overpass and into the Glebe. Here stores still fronted Bank Street, but the blocks running east and west on either side were all residential. When she crossed Lansdowne Bridge, she turned east by the Public Library, following Echo Drive down to Riverdale, crossed Riverdale and walked down Avenue Road until she eventually reached Windsor Park.

Her route took her in the opposite direction from her apartment on Ossington, but she liked the peaceful mood of the park at night. The Rideau River moved sluggishly to her left. The grass was still wet underfoot, soaking her sneakers. The brisk walk from downtown Ottawa had warmed her up so that her teeth no longer chattered. The night was quiet and she was sober enough to indulge in one of her favorite pastimes: looking in through the lit windows of the houses she passed to catch brief glimpses of other people's lives.

Other people's lives. Did other people's boyfriends leave them because they were too dull?

She'd met Will at her sister Connie's wedding three months ago. He'd been charmed then, by the same things that had sent him storming out of her life earlier this evening. Then it had been "a relief to find someone who isn't just into image." A person who "valued the quiet times." Now she was boring because she wouldn't do *anything*. But he was the one who'd changed.

When they first met, they'd made their own good times, not needing an endless tour of parties and bars. But quiet times at home weren't enough for Will anymore, while she hadn't wanted a change. Had that really been what she'd wanted, she asked herself now, or was she just too lazy to do more?

She hadn't been able to answer that earlier, and she couldn't answer it now. How did other people deal with this kind of thing?

She looked in back yards and windows, as if expecting to find an answer there. The houses that fronted Belmont Avenue and backed onto the park where she was walking were mostly brick or wood-frame, dating back to the fifties and earlier. She moved catlike in the grass beside them, not going too close to the lit windows, not even stepping into their back yards, just stealing her glimpses as she moved slowly by. Here an overhead fixture lit a huge oil painting of a Maritime fishing village, there subtle lighting gleamed on two marble statues of birds—an eagle and an owl, the light behind them hiding their features, if not their profiles, and making soft halos around their silhouettes.

She paused, smiling at the picture they made, feeling almost sober. She moved on, then tensed, hearing a sound in the distance. It was a deep-throated growl of a sound that she couldn't quite place.

She looked around the park, then to the house beside the one with the two marble birds. Its windows were dark, but she had the feeling that someone was standing there, looking out at her as quietly as she was looking in. Catsoft. Silent against the rumble of sound that was getting louder, steadily approaching. For a long moment she returned the gaze of the hidden watcher. She swayed and shivered, sobriety and warmth leaving as she paused too long in one spot. Then she caught a glimpse of movement at the far end of the park.

It looked like a young boy—no more than ten or twelve, judging from his size, though she knew that could be deceptive in the dark. He ran under a pool of shadows thrown by the trees near the river, came out of them again, disappeared into another splash of darkness. And then the sound was all around her. She stood stunned at its volume.

It was the roar of an engine, she realized. No. Make that engines. Her gaze was drawn back to the far end of the park where the boy had first appeared and she picked out the source of the deep-throated roaring.

One by one the Harleys came into view until there were nine of the big chopped-down machines moving down the concrete walkway that followed the river. Jacky gasped when they left the concrete. Their tires ripped up the wet sod. They

were coming towards her, the thunder of their engines un-
believably loud, their riders black featureless shapes.

She stumbled backwards, looking for a place to hide, and
came up short against a cedar hedge. Her heart drummed a
sharp tattoo in her chest. Then she saw that they weren't after
her. It was the boy. She'd forgotten the boy. . . .

He was running across the grass now, the nine bikes following in a fanned-out half-circle, engines growling. Jacky
vacillated between fear for the boy and her own panic. She
shot a glance at the window of the house behind her and saw
the hidden watcher clearly for a moment. A tall man, standing there in the safety of his house, watching. . . .

She turned back, saw the boy stumble, the bikers closing
in. They were frightening shapes in the dim light, not quite
defined. Growling beasts with shadow riders. They circled
around the fallen boy, a grotesque merry-go-rounding blur
with whining engine coughs in place of a calliope's music,
until something snapped in Jacky.

"No!" she cried.

If the bikers could hear her above the roar of their machines, they gave no notice. Jacky ran towards them, slipping
drunkenly on the grass, wondering why there weren't lights
going on all up and down the block behind her, why there
was only one man watching from his window, a silent shape
in his dark house.

Around and around the bikers rode their machines, tightening the circumference of their circle, until they finally
brought their machines to skidding halts. Sod spat from their
rear wheels as all nine Harleys turned to face the boy. The
riders fed gas to their machines so that they lunged forward
like impatient dogs, hungry for the kill, held back only by
the leather-gloved grips on the brake levers.

The boy rose in a crouch, speared by the beams of nine
headlights. And it wasn't a boy, Jacky saw suddenly. It was
a man—a little man no taller than a child, with a tuft of white
hair at his chin, and more spilling out from under a red cap.
He had a short wooden staff in his hand that he brandished
at the bikers. His eyes glowed red in the headbeams of the
Harleys, like a fox's or a cat's.

She saw all this in just one moment, the space between
one breath and the next, then her sneakers slipped on the wet

grass underfoot and she went sprawling. Adrenaline burned
through her, bringing her to her feet with a grace and speed
she wouldn't have been able to muster sober, that she
shouldn't have at all, drunk as she was. She saw the little
man charge the bikers.

A spark of light leapt from the leader of the black-clad
riders. It made a circuit of each biker, crackling from hand
to hand until it returned to the leader. Then it arced out and
the staff exploded. Not one of the riders had moved, but the
staff hung in splinters from the little man's hand. A second
spark made its circuit, darting from the leader to the little
man. He stiffened, dancing on the spot as though he was
being electrocuted, then he crumpled and fell to the ground
in a limp heap. Jacky reached the closest biker at the same
time.

As she reached out to grab the black-leather clad arm, the
man turned. She looked for his face under his helmet, but
there seemed to be nothing there. Only shadow, hidden by
the smoked glass of a visor. She stumbled back as the rider
twisted the accelerator control of his bike. The machine answered with a deep-throated growl and the bike pulled away.

One by one they moved out, the roar of their loud engines
dwindling as they drew away. Jacky watched them return the
way they'd come. She hugged herself, shaking. Then they
were gone, around the corner, out of sight. The sound of the
machines should have remained, but it too was cut off abruptly
as the last machine disappeared from view.

Jacky took a step towards the little man. His head lay at
an impossible angle, neck broken. Dead. She swallowed
thickly, throat dry. She looked at the backs of the houses.
There was still no sign that anyone in them had heard a thing.
She hesitated, looking from the houses back to the broken
body of the little man.

His cap had fallen when he'd collapsed, coming to rest not
far from her feet. She picked it up. A man's dead, she thought.
Those bikers. . . . She remembered what she'd seen behind
that one visor. Nothing. Shadow. But that had been because
of the smoked glass. That had been just . . . her own fear.
The shock of the moment.

She swallowed again, then started for the house where she'd
seen the tall man watching. He'd be her witness that the bik-

ers had been there. That she wasn't just imagining what had
happened. But when she reached the back yard of that house,
the building had an empty look to it. She looked to her right.
There were the two marble birds. She looked back. This house
was deserted, its yard overgrown with weeds. No one lived
here. There hadn't been anyone watching. . . .

She shook her head. It was all starting to catch up with
her now. The drinks. The shock of what she'd just witnessed.
Her stupidity at just rushing in. It was all because of the
weird head-trip she'd fallen into when Will had walked out
. . . about being empty . . . and cutting her hair. . . . She
ran her fingers through the uneven thatch on her head. That
much was real. Slowly she made her way back to where the
little man's body lay.

There was nothing there. No dead little man. No tracks
where the Harleys had torn up the sod. There was only the
splintered staff and what looked like. . . . She knelt down
and reached out a hand. Ashes. A scatter of ashes. That was
all that was left of the little man. Ashes and a splintered staff
and. . . . She brought up her other hand and looked down at
the cap. And this.

CHAPTER
2

Jacky stayed home from work the next day. She was too hung over to go in, too embarrassed by her ragged hair, too exhausted after spending a night on her couch, dozing fitfully, waking from dreams filled with faceless bikers driving machines that were like wheeled dragons, who were looking for her. . . .

She spent the day going from her mirror to cleaning the apartment; from the mirror to stare at the strange red cap; from the mirror to force some toast and coffee into a queasy stomach; from the mirror to the toilet bowl where she lost the toast. She took a shower, but it didn't help. Finally, late in the day, she slept, not waking until midnight.

This time the toast stayed down, so she made herself some soup, ate it, and it stayed down as well. She stayed away from the mirror, hid the cap on the top shelf of her hall closet, and sat up watching Edward G. Robinson in *The Last Gangster* on the late show until she fell asleep again. But when she woke the next morning, she still couldn't face going to work.

It wasn't just her hair or the dissatisfaction that Will had awoken in her. She wasn't even afraid of what she'd seen—imagined?—the previous night in the park. It was a combination of it all that left her realizing that things just weren't right with her world. She'd often seen herself as a round peg that everyone was trying to fit into a square hole. Her parents, her sister, Will, her co-workers . . . maybe even herself. Now she realized that she was more like a bit of scruffy flotsam, not moving against the flow as she'd liked to think privately, but just going wherever the flow pushed her. The path of least resistance. And it wasn't right.

She phoned in to work and put in for some time off that was owed to her. Her boss wasn't happy about giving it to her—things were behind schedule, but then things were always behind schedule—but he gave it to her all the same. She had three weeks. Three weeks that she could use sitting in her apartment waiting for her hair to grow while she tried to decide what was important in her life, important to her, at least, if to no one else, something that could be articulated so that she didn't have to have that helpless, hopeless feeling again that she'd had when Will tore into her last night.

She meant well, but her energy level was simply too low. It was all she could do to just sit on the sofa and alternate staring at mindless soap operas and game shows with gazing out the window. The phone rang a few times, but she ignored it. By the time the doorbell sounded around five, she felt so lethargic that she almost left it unanswered as well, except that the doorbell was followed by a sharp rapping which, in turn, was followed by a familiar voice shouting through the door's wooden panels.

"If you don't open this door, Jacqueline Rowan, I swear I'll kick it down!"

Jacky started guiltily and jumped up from the couch. Forgetting how she looked, with her cornstraw hair poking up at odd angles from every part of her head and her eyes still swollen and red, she went to unlock the door.

"I swear," Kate said as she came pushing in, "someday you're going to give me a—oh, Jacky. What have you *done* to your hair?"

Kate Hazel was Jacky's oldest and best friend. She was a small woman with a narrow face and a head of short dark curls who always seemed enviably slim to Jacky. At a few inches taller than Kate's five foot one, Jacky carried at least ten more pounds than her friend did—"All in the right places," Kate would tease her, but that didn't make Jacky feel any better about it. They'd met in high school, shared their first joint together in Kate's parents' garage, lost their virginity at the same time—the week before their high school graduation—gone to Europe together for one summer, and stayed fast friends through every kind of scrape to the present day.

Jacky moved back from Kate until there was a wall behind her and she couldn't go any further.

"I was worried sick," Kate said. "I tried calling you at work, and then here, and. . . ." She paused for a breath and stared at Jacky's short unruly spikes of hair again. "What's happened to you, Jacky?"

"Nothing."

"But look at your hair."

"It just . . . happened."

"Just *happened*? Give me a break. It looks awful—like someone hacked away at it with a pair of garden shears."

"That's kind of how it happened."

Kate steered Jacky into the living room and onto the sofa. Perching beside her, back against a fat cushioned arm, legs pulled up to her chest, she put an expectant look on her face and asked, "Well? Are you going to give me all the sordid details or what?"

Jacky sighed, half wishing that she'd never answered the door, but she was stuck with it now. And this *was* Kate after all. Clearing her throat, she began to speak.

She left out what had happened in the park last night, telling Kate only about Will's walking out on her, about standing in front of the mirror, about getting drunk—("Well, I don't blame you," Kate remarked. "I'd do the same if I saw that looking back at me from the mirror.")—and how she hadn't been able to go to work for the past two days and probably wouldn't until she'd done *something* about it.

Kate nodded sympathetically through it all. "You're better off without Will," she said at the end. "I always thought there was something glossy about him—you know, all shine, but no substance."

"You never said that to me."

"And you were all set to listen? Honestly, Jacky. When you get those stars in your eyes you don't want to hear anything but sweet nothings—and you don't want to hear them from me."

Jacky reached up a hand to twist nervously at her hair, but

the long locks weren't there. She dropped her hand to her lap and covered it with the other. She knew Kate was just trying to kid her out of feeling bad, but she couldn't stop her lower lip from trembling. She didn't dare say anything more, didn't want to even be sitting here, because in another minute she was just going to fall to pieces.

Kate suddenly realized just that. "I'm sorry, Jacky," she said. "I was being flippant."

"It's not that. I just . . . when he . . ."

Words dissolved into a flood of tears. Kate held Jacky's head against her shoulder and murmured quietly until Jacky stopped shaking. Then she pulled a crumpled Kleenex from her pocket and offered it over.

"It's not really used," she said. "It just looks that way."

Jacky blew her nose, then wiped her eyes on the sleeve of her shirt.

"I didn't know you were that big on Will," Kate went on. "I mean, I knew you liked him and all, but I didn't think it was this serious."

"It . . . it's not really Will," Jacky said. "It's everything. I don't do anything. I'm not anybody. All I do is go to work and then hang around the apartment. I see you, I saw Will, and that was it."

"Well, what is it that you want to do?" Kate asked.

"I don't know. Something. Anything. Can you think of anything?"

She looked hopefully at Kate, but Kate only sighed and leaned back against the arm of the sofa again.

"I don't know what to say," Kate finally said. "Are you sure you're not just overreacting to what Will said? I mean, *I* always thought you were happy."

"I don't know if I was happy or not. I feel so empty now— and it's not from Will's leaving me. It's like I just discovered I have a hole inside me and now that I know it's there, it's going to hurt until I fill it."

Kate pulled her oversized purse from the floor beside the sofa. "At the risk of sounding facetious," she said, "I bought some sticky buns on the way over. One of them with a hot tea could help to fill up at least an empty stomach, dearie."

The last part of what she said was delivered in a quavery old lady's voice that tugged a smile from Jacky.

"Perfect," Jacky said. "I'm worrying about how I look, and all you can think of is fattening me up."

"This is food for the soul," Kate insisted in a hurt voice. "I thought you were speaking of soulish type things. I didn't realize that you were just hungry."

"I suppose if I became a blimp, no one would notice my hair."

"What a romantic notion: my blimpy friend, floating through the night skies in search of—what? More sticky buns? I say you, nay! She searches for the perfect hairdresser—one who combines aerobics with hairstyling."

That lifted a genuine laugh from Jacky and soon they were in her kitchen, drinking tea and finishing off the sticky buns. As it got close to seven, Kate had to beg off.

"I promised my mom I'd stop by tonight—but I won't be staying late. Come by later if you don't want to be by yourself. In fact, come along. Mom'll be so shocked by your hair that she'll totally forget to nag me."

"Not a chance," Jacky told her.

"You're probably right. You sure you'll be okay?"

Jacky nodded. "Thanks for coming by."

"Anytime. And listen, Jacky. Don't try to take on everything all at once—okay? One thing at a time. You can't force yourself to get new interests. They've just got to come. I guess the trick is to stay open to them. Maybe we could look into taking some courses together or something—what do you think?"

"That sounds great."

"Okay. Now I've really got to run. Promise me you won't cut off anything else until you've at least talked to me first?"

Jacky aimed a kick at her, but Kate was already out the door and laughing down the stairs.

"I'll get you for that!" Jacky called after her.

She closed the door quickly to make sure she got the last word in, but her satisfied grin faded as she turned to confront the apartment. In the space of a moment, it seemed far too small, now that Kate was gone. The good feelings that Kate had left with her went spiralling away. The walls felt as though they were leaning towards her, closing in. The ceiling sinking, the floor rising.

She had to get out, Jacky realized. Just for some fresh air, if nothing else.

Opening the door to her hall closet, she reached up to take her blue quilted cotton jacket from its peg and the red cap she'd found two nights previously fell into her hands. She turned it over, fingering its rough cloth. She hadn't told Kate about this. Not about the empty house with its hidden watcher. Not about the bikers. Not about the little dead man. Was it because she still wasn't sure if anything had really happened?

But the cap was here, in her hands. No matter what else she might or might not have imagined, there was still the cap. It was real.

"I don't even want to think about this," she said, shutting the closet door.

Stuffing the cap into the pocket of her jacket, she went down the stairs and out into the growing night. She tried hard to just enjoy the brisk evening air, but the mystery of last night's odd little scenario played over and over again in her mind no matter how much she tried to ignore it, intensifying with each repetition. It had to have been more than a drunken illusion. There *was* the cap, after all. But if it was real, then she'd seen a murder. Bikers killing a little old man. Bikers without faces. A corpse that disappeared.

Finally she turned her steps in the direction of Windsor Park. Whatever had or hadn't happened there, she had to see the place again. It was that, or accept that she was going completely off the deep end . . .

CHAPTER
3

Windsor Park had none of the feel of otherworldly menace tonight as it had had two nights ago when her fears and— vision? Drunken hallucination?—had sent her fleeing from its shadowed boundaries. There was still a mystery in the darkness, but it was the same mystery that could be found in any night—the stars up high, the whisper of a wind, the dark buildings with their lighted windows and the glimpses of all those other lives through them.

She paused in front of the deserted house. As she looked at its dark bulk, the flood of last night's images that had been troubling her washed away. God, she could be so stupid sometimes. Bad enough she'd hacked off all of her hair and then went out and got drunker than she'd been since she and Kate had celebrated their first pay cheques. Or that she'd let Will get her so worked up about what she did with her life. But then she'd had to manufacture this whole . . . weirdness involving men staring at her from empty houses, biker gangs and little men. . . .

She pulled the cap from her pocket and investigated it, more by feel than by sight. But there was still this cap, she thought. She had to talk to Kate about it. Right. And she had to get on with her life. First thing tomorrow she'd go to the hairdresser's and have something done about this mess she'd made of her hair. When people asked her why she was wearing it short now, she'd tell them it was because she wanted it this way. It had been time for a change, that was all. Time to find some . . . meaning.

That brought a frown. She brushed the short stubble with her fingers. She wished Will had kept his opinions to himself.

Still fingering the cap, she stretched it between her hands, wondering if it would fit. It would hide the ruin of her hair. She put it on, then blinked. A quick sensation of vertigo almost made her lose her balance. When she recovered, the night had changed on her again.

The otherworldly feeling was back. The silence. The cat-soft sense of something waiting. She turned to look at the empty house and saw him again, the watcher, standing at his window, studying the night, looking at her, beyond her. She turned to look out at the park where he was looking.

It had either grown lighter, or her night vision was sharper tonight. She could see straight into the heavy shadows under the trees by the river, see the splayed branches, each leaf and each bough, and there. . . . She sucked in a quick breath. Sitting silent on his Harley was one of last night's riders—a black figure on his black and chrome machine, a shadow watching her as well.

There was a connection between the riders and the man in the house. She knew that now. She didn't quite dare approach the rider—last night's wild plunge from her hiding place had been an act of bravado that she wasn't prepared to repeat sober—but the watcher in the house might not be beyond her. She could call to him, talk to him through the windows. She started to push her way through the low cedar hedge.

"Hsssst!"

She turned quickly, looking left and right. Nothing. A pinprick of fear snuck up her spine. Before she could move again, a low voice sounded almost in her ear.

"Don't be so quick to visit the Gruagagh of Kinrowan—there's some say he owes as much loyalty to the Unseelie Court as he does to his own Laird."

This time she looked up. There was a small man perched in the branches of an oak tree that grew on the border of the park and the back yard of the watcher's house. She could see him very clearly, his blue jacket and the red cap on his head like the one she was wearing. He had a grim sort of face, a craggy expanse between his beard and cap, nose like a hawk, quick feral eyes.

"Who . . .?" she began, but her throat was too dry and the word came out as a croak.

"Dunrobin Finn's a name I'll answer to. Here. Take my hand." He reached down a gnarled hand, veins pronounced, the knuckles knobbly.

Jacky hesitated.

"Quick now," Finn said. "Or do you want to be the Big Man's supper?" He pointed in the direction of the rider as he spoke.

"Do . . . do you mean the biker?" Jacky managed.

Finn laughed mirthlessly. Before Jacky knew what he was up to, he was down on the ground beside her. He hoisted her up under one arm and scrambled back up the tree. She was shocked at his speed and his strength, and clung desperately to the trunk of the tree when he set her on a perch, her legs dangling below her. It was a long way down.

"That one," Finn said, "is one of the Wild Hunt, and you don't have to be afraid of them until all nine are gathered." He pointed again. "There's the Big Man—Gyre the Younger."

Jacky's gaze followed his finger and she drew in a sharp breath. Standing with his back to them, facing the river, was a man who had to be at least eighteen feet tall. He was close to the trees that rimmed the riverbank and she'd taken his legs for tree trunks, never looking higher. Dizzy now, she clung harder to the tree she was in.

"Where . . . where are we, Dunrobin?" she asked.

It still looked like Windsor Park, but with giants and little gnome men in trees, it had to be a Windsor Park in an Ottawa that wasn't her own.

"Dunrobin's my clan name—it's Finn you should be calling me. That's the way we hobs pair our names—at least our speaking names. And this is still your own world. You're just seeing it through different eyes, seeing how you're wearing a hob's spellcap and all."

"It doesn't feel like my world anymore," Jacky said slowly.

"There *are* Otherworlds," Finn said; "but they're not for the likes of us. We're newcomers, you know. The Other-

worlds belong to those whose land this was before we came—
same as our own Middle Kingdom in the homeland belongs
to us. Now that cap you're wearing—it belonged to Redfairn
Tom. I know him, for he's a cousin, on my father's side.
Where did you get it?''

"I. . . ."

She didn't know what to say. What she'd seen two nights
ago . . . If she'd tried telling anyone about it, they'd have
looked at her like she wasn't playing with a full deck. But
this little man . . . He'd believe. The problem was, she wasn't
all that sure that he was real himself. God, it was confusing.

"Give me your jacket while you're telling the tale."

She looked at him. "What?"

"Your jacket. I'll stitch a spell or two into it while we're
talking. Walking around like you are, anybody can see you
plain as day. The Host is strong now—getting stronger every
day. They see you wearing a hob's redcap and they'll just as
soon spike you as ask you the time of day. Come, come.
You've a shirt on, as I can plainly see, and it's not so cold.
Best give me your shoes while you're at it.''

"Please," Jacky said. "I don't understand what's going
on."

"Well, that's plain to see, walking about in the Big Man's
shadow with never a care. Planning on calling in on Kinrowan's wizard and not a charm on you but a redcap and while
that'll let you *see*, it won't mean a damn if he decides to find
out what sort of a toad you'd make—do you follow my meaning?''

"I . . . No. No, I don't.''

"Well, what don't you understand? And do give me that
jacket. All we need now is for the Big Man to turn around
and see you sitting here, like a chicken in its roost, waiting
for him to pluck it.''

"I don't understand anything. This Kinrowan you're talking about—my name's Rowan, too." She took off her jacket
as she spoke, warily balancing herself on her branch, and
passed it over.

"Is it now? That's a lucky name, named for a lucky tree,
red-berried and all. Red berry, amber and red thread—now
that's a charm that would stop even a bogan, you know. Do
you have just the one speaking name?''

She shook her head. "It's Jacqueline Elizabeth Rowan—but my friends just call me Jacky. What's a speaking name?"

"They're usually boys," Finn said to himself.

"What?"

"Nothing." He had just produced a needle and thread and was stitching a design on the inside of her jacket, the gnarled fingers moving deftly and quick. "A speaking name's the one you'll let others speak aloud, you know? As opposed to your real name that you keep hidden—the one that a gruagagh can use to make spells with."

"I don't have a secret name—just the one I told you."

"Oh? Well, you best keep the rest of your name to yourself in future, Jacky Rowan. You never know who's listening, if you get my meaning." He looked up from his work and fixed her with a glare that, she supposed, was meant to convey his seriousness. What it did do was succeed in frightening her.

"I . . . I'll remember that."

"Good. Now let's start again. The cap. Where did you get Tom's cap?"

Watching him stitch, Jacky told him all that she'd seen—or thought she'd seen—two nights ago. Finn paused when she was done and shook his head.

"Oh, that's bad," he said. "That's very bad. Poor Tom. He was a kind old hob and never a moment's trouble. I didn't know him well, but my brother used to gad about with him." He sighed, then looked at her. "and it's bad for you, too, Jacky Rowan. They've marked you now."

Jacky leaned forward and lost her balance. She would have tumbled to the ground if Finn hadn't shot out a gnarled hand and plucked her from the air. He set her back down on her branch and gave her a quick grin that was more unhappy than cheerful. It did nothing to set her at ease.

"Who . . . who's marked me?"

"The Host—the Unseelie Court, who else? Why do you think I'm talking to you, girl? Why do you think I'm helping you? I'd sooner take a crack in the head from a big stick before letting anyone fall into their clutches."

"You've mentioned them before. Who or what are they?"

Finn tied off the last stitch on her jacket and passed it over. "Put this on first and give me your shoes."

"What did you do to my jacket?" she asked.

"Stitched a hob spell into it. Now when you're wearing it, mortals won't see you at all, day or night, and neither will faerie, not the Laird's folk, nor the Host." He took her sneakers as she passed them to him, one by one, and went on. "Now the Laird's folk—those who follow Kinrowan's banner here—are sometimes called the Seelie Court. That comes from the old language, you know, and it means happy or blessed. But the Unseelie Court is made up of bogans and the sluagh—the restless dead—and other grim folk.

"We followed you here, followed your forefathers when they first came to these shores. Then we shared the land with the spirits who were here first, until they withdrew into their Otherworlds and left this world to us. We live in the cities mostly, close to men, for it's said we depend on their belief to keep us hale. I don't know how true that tale is, but time has played its mischief on us and we dwindle now—at least the Laird's folk do—while those of the Unseelie Court—oh, there's scarce a day goes by that doesn't strengthen them."

"But I don't know *anybody* who believes in any of you," Jacky protested.

"Now, that's where you're wrong. There's few that believe in the Laird's folk, that's too true, but the Host. . . . I've seen the books you read, the movies you see. They speak of the undead and of every horror that ever served in Gyre the Elder's Court. Your people might not say they believe when you ask them, but just their reading those books, watching those movies. . . . Jacky Rowan, every time they do, they strengthen our enemy and make us weak.

"We're few and very few now, while the Host has never been stronger. They're driving us from the cities and you've seen the Big Man yourself, just standing there, waiting for Kinrowan's Gruagagh to fall, if he hasn't already sold his soul to them. It's a bad time for us, Jacky Rowan. And a bad time for you, too, for now they've marked you as well."

"Marked me as what?" she asked.

"As one of us."

He was stitching designs on the insides of her sneakers now, first one, then the other, reminding her of all the stories that her mother had read to her of fairy tailors and shoemakers.

"But I'm not one of you," she said.

"Doesn't make no differ—not to them."

"Then the bikers . . . they'll be after me?"

Finn shrugged. "I don't know. These'll help," he added, holding up a sneaker. "I'm stitching swiftness into them. You'll run so fast now that even a Big Man'll have trouble catching you. But the Wild Hunt? I don't know. Not yet. But soon, perhaps."

"They're part of the Unseelie Court, too?"

"No. But Gyre the Elder has the Horn that commands them, so when he bids them fetch, they fetch. When he bids them kill, they kill. They must obey the Horn."

He was quiet then, concentrating on his work. Jacky peeked at the biker through the leaves, but she wouldn't look at the bulk of the giant keeping silent watch on something across the river.

"There's seven of those giants in this Unseelie Court," Finn said suddenly, "and each one's nastier than the one before. Just the two Gyres and Thundell are here now, but the rest are coming. They want the Gruagagh's Tower first, for there's power in it. And then they'll want the Heart of Kinrowan. And then—why then, they'll have it all, Jacky Rowan. You and me and every seelie one of us there be, damn their stone hearts!"

"But can't . . . can't you stop them?"

"Me? What am I to do? Or any of the Laird's folk? We're weak, Jacky Rowan—I told you that. We're not strong enough to stop them anymore. Now we must just hide and watch and hope we can stay out of their way. Pray that they don't find the Laird and spike his heart. But we don't have much hope. The time of heroes is long gone now."

"But what about the Gruagagh?" she asked, stumbling over the word.

"Well, now." Finn finished the second of her sneakers and passed them over to her. "He's a queer one, he is. A Kinrowan as well, on his mother's side, but there's not a one of us that trusts him now, and there's nothing he can do anyway."

"Why? What did he do?"

"No one knows for sure, but it's said he turned the Laird's daughter over to Gyre the Elder."

"Did he?"

"I don't know, Jacky Rowan. He was escorting her home to the Hill, just the two of them, you know, and the next thing we know, she's gone and we find him on the road, hurt some, but not dead. Now you tell me: would they let him live if he wasn't one of their own?"

"I . . . I don't know."

"No one does."

"What happened to the Laird's daughter?" Jacky asked.

"No one knows that either. Some say Gyre the Elder ate her. Others say he's got her locked away somewhere, but no one knows where. The Wild Hunt could find her, but Gyre the Elder's got the Horn, so only he can command them."

"You should get the Horn then," Jacky said. "Couldn't the Gruagagh get it for you?"

"The Gruagagh can't leave his Tower," Finn said. "That's the only place he's safe. And he must be protected for the way to the Laird is through him, you see."

Jacky didn't and said so.

"In peaceful times," Finn replied, "the Gruagagh sees to the welfare of Kinrowan itself. He sits in his Tower, weaving and braiding the threads of luck that flow through the earth by the will of the Moon—ley lines. Do you know what I mean?"

"Vaguely. I mean, I've heard of leys before."

"Yes. Well, his Tower. . . . Think of it as a great loom that he uses to gather the luck we need, the luck that he weaves into the fabric of the realm. When there's a snag or tear in the luck threads, it's the Gruagagh who solves the problem, sometimes by a simple spell to untangle a knot in the thread, other times by directing the hobs and brownies of the Court to remove the obstruction. The luck gave us life and sustains us, you see, while the tides of your belief strengthens or weakens what we already are—at least that's what I heard the Laird say once. He said that without the lines of luck, we would be wholly dependent upon your belief and soon gone from this world.

"So the Gruagagh sees to the physical realm and its boundaries, while the Court itself and its people are looked after by our Laird and his family. The Laird rules and settles disputes, while his lady and her daughters hold in trust the songs that sow the seeds deeper, make the harvests more bountiful, keep the Host at bay on Samhaine Eve—the day-by-day magics that make life better. Only now our Laird is widowed and his daughter's gone. . . ."

Finn's voice trailed off and he looked at Jacky. He seemed surprised by her attentiveness. "Are you sure you want to hear all of this?" he asked.

"Oh, yes," Jacky said.

It was like being caught up in a fairy tale, she thought. She imagined this Laird's daughter, maybe captive somewhere—if she was still alive—and all that was keeping her going was the hope that her father, or one of his people, would rescue her. And the Gruagagh—he was already a tragic figure in her mind.

"Well," Finn said. "Things being as they are—with the Laird widowed and his daughter lost—there's no one but the Gruagagh to do both jobs, to protect both the realm and its people so he has to stay in his Tower. The Host can't breach the Tower, but the Gruagagh must remain in it, for if he ventures forth again now and they catch him, then Kinrowan's fate is sealed and the Seelie Court will rule here no more."

"I don't understand why no one trusts him," Jacky said. "It sounds to me like he's doing his job."

"There's those who think he's only waiting until the time is right, and then he'll hand us all over to the Host—as he did with the Laird's daughter."

"Then why don't you get a new gruagagh?"

Finn sighed. "Because he's all we have—there's no one else to be had. But it's hard to trust a man who keeps so much of himself to himself."

"So what you really need is to get the Laird's daughter back," Jacky said. "Would he know what to do?"

"Would who know?"

"This Gruagagh of yours—would he know how to find the Horn?"

Finn started to answer her, then shook his head. He gave a quick look to the deserted house behind them. When his gaze returned to her, his eyes were troubled.

"I don't know," he said. "No one's asked him."

"Why not?"

Finn looked away then, refusing to meet her gaze.

"Why not?" she repeated.

"Because," he said finally, "there's few that would chance
a talk with the Gruagagh—after what happened to the Laird's
daughter, even the Laird avoids him. And there's no one who'd
dare go looking for the Horn." His gaze returned to hers and
he flinched at the look in her eyes. "Would you?" he demanded.

"Me? Why should I? She's not *my* Laird's daughter."

"But you're kin—you said so yourself. Your name's
Rowan."

"Finn, until tonight, I never heard of *any* of you."

"Well then, you see," he said. "You're no different from
the rest of us. You won't go, and neither will we, and all for
the same reason no matter what we say. It's because we don't
have the courage."

Now it was Jacky's turn to flinch. For one moment she was
back in her apartment and Will was slamming the door.

"This is stupid," she said. "None of this is even real."

"Oh?" Finn asked, glaring at her. "Then why don't you
waltz over to yon' Big Man and give him a kick in the toe.
See what he has to say, before he swallows you whole!"

"The Big Man isn't even there and neither are you. I'm
just seeing you both because of this stupid cap."

"It's because of the cap that you finally do *see*. We're all
around you all the time, Jacky Rowan. Though in a few years
time, it'll be only the Unseelie Court that walks the twilight
shades of your world. Wear that cap long enough and you
won't need it to *see* anymore. But then . . . oh, then. . . .
Merriment will have fled and all the wonder. There'll be
nothing left but the Host and I wish you well in that world!"

She matched him, glare for glare; then before he could
make a move she was sliding down the tree and running for
the house that Finn had called the Gruagagh's Tower. She
moved so fast, thanks to whatever magics that the hob had
stitched into her sneakers, that she was at the back door before he was even down the tree.

"I'll show you!" she cried to him. Turning, she hammered
on the door.

"Jacky Rowan, no!" Finn cried.

He knew what she couldn't, that the Gruagagh was quick
to anger; that he had real power, not the small skilly stitcheries of a hob; that if he was roused in anger she would regret

it for all the short minutes that remained in her life. But he was too late. The door opened and the Gruagagh was there, tall and forbidding in the doorway. Finn saw Jacky take a half-step back, then square her shoulders and look up at him.

"Mr. Gruagagh," he heard her say. "Can we talk?"

Finn sped across the yard, but the door closed behind them before he reached it. He lifted a hand to knock himself, hesitated, then let it fall back down to his side. For a long time he stared at the door's wooden slats, then slowly he returned to his perch in the oak tree. He sat there, staring out over the park, at the Big Man and the solitary member of the Wild Hunt. He thought of his cousin, Redfairn Tom, of what had happened to him, and he shivered.

"It's all gone bad," he muttered to himself. "Oh, very bad."

CHAPTER
4

Jacky followed the Gruagagh inside. Moonlight came in through the window looking out on the park, throwing a vague light on what appeared to be a kitchen, only its furnishings seemed vague and insubstantial, shifting and changing as she looked around. One moment the shadowy bulk of a refrigerator was by the door, the next it was over by the sink, and then it didn't exist at all. Ghostly stoves, kitchen tables and chairs, cupboards and counters came and went, never present long enough to quite focus on. In the darker corners where the moonlight didn't reach, there were rustlings and stirrings, as though small hidden creatures were disturbed by their entrance.

The Gruagagh lit a candle with a snap of his fingers and the darker shadows vanished. There was nothing in them. There were no ghostly furnishings. The room was empty except for the two of them. Jacky swallowed thickly. Just a trick, she told herself. But now the flickering light banished the shadows from the Gruagagh's face, and she wasn't so sure if it being a trick or not made any difference.

If Finn had seemed a little grim at first, the Gruagagh radiated a forbidding power that made Jacky wish she'd stayed outside in the hob's tree. His eyes were a piercing blue and he would have been a handsome man except for the scar that marked the whole left side of his face, puckering the skin.

25

"They did that . . . didn't they?" she said, looking at the scar. "The Unseelie Court . . ."

He made no reply. Instead, he sat down in the windowseat that commanded a view of Windsor Park and gazed outside, into the darkness. There was no place for Jacky to sit. She shifted her weight from foot to foot, wondering what had possessed her to come here. The Gruagagh scared her without making a move, without saying a word—and he was one of the good guys. She hoped. She cleared her throat and he looked away from the window, back to her.

"Why are you here?" he asked.

His voice was gravelly and low, not cold, but not exactly friendly either. Jacky tried a quick smile, but the set expression of his features didn't change. He waited for her reply. He looked as though he could sit there and wait forever.

"I . . . I want to help," Jacky managed at last.

The Gruagagh smiled humourlessly. "What can you do?" he asked. "Can you command the Wild Hunt? Are you a giant-killer? Or perhaps you mean to spirit us all away to some safe haven?"

Jacky took a quick step back under the vehemence in his voice. She remembered Finn saying something about being turned into a toad and her knees began to go weak.

"I don't know what I can do," she said finally. "But at least . . . at least I'm willing to try."

The Gruagagh said nothing for a long time. He returned his gaze to the park, frowning.

"That's true," he said. "And one should never ignore aid when it's offered, even by such a—" He looked her up and down. "—such a tatterdemalion."

"I didn't know this was supposed to be a fashion pageant," Jacky began, then put her knuckles to her mouth.

She hadn't meant to come out with that. She flinched as the Gruagagh lifted his arm, but he only patted the windowseat.

"Don't be afraid," he said. "That's twice I've spoken out of turn, and twice I've deserved a reprimand. What do they call you?" he added as Jacky cautiously made her way to the windowseat.

She sat as far from him as the seat would allow.

"Jacky," she said. "Jacky Rowan."

The Gruagagh nodded. "I see now," he said.

"What? What do you see?"

"Why you've come, for one thing. You've a lucky name and are kin as well."

"What's your name?" she asked, then corrected herself. "I mean, what's your speaking name? Or does everyone just call you the Gruagagh?"

"No one speaks to me at all," he said. "Except for the night. And it whispers with the voices of the sluagh. But my friends, when I had them, called me Bhruic Dearg."

Jacky nodded. "Is Bhruic your clan name?" She pronounced it "Vrooick," trying to approximate the way he'd said it.

"You've been talking to hobs," he said. "No. My clan is that of Kinrowan, the same as the Laird, though he's not so likely to own to that as he once was. Bhruic Dearg is my bardic name—Dearg for the rowan's red berries. I was a bard before I was a gruagagh—but that was long ago now, too."

"What . . . what should I call you?" she asked.

"Bhruic, if you wish."

"All right." She tried a small smile but the Gruagagh merely studied her.

"How did you mean to help us?" he asked finally.

Jacky's smile died. "It's. . . ." She paused and began again. "Finn told me about . . . about the Laird's daughter . . ." She glanced at him, saw his eyes darken with shadows. She went on quickly. "I thought if we could retrieve the Horn—the Wild Hunt's Horn—we could use them to find her and then, then we could rescue her . . . if . . . "

"If she lives." The Gruagagh finished the sentence where Jacky didn't quite dare.

"Oh, I'm sure she's okay," Jacky said. "She's got to be."

"There," the Gruagagh said, "speaks one who doesn't know the Unseelie Court as we do."

"But if she is alive . . ."

The Gruagagh sighed. "Even if she is alive, she might be changed. . . ."

"What do you mean?"

"When the Host catch one of the Laird's folk . . . if they don't kill them outright, they change them. They diminish

their light . . . their goodness . . . and make them over into
their own kind.''

"Then we've got to try and do something!"

Jacky wasn't sure why she was so caught up with the fate
of the Laird's daughter. She just knew it was important. Not
just to the Laird's folk, but for herself as well. It held . . .
meaning.

"Do you know where the Horn is?" she asked.

The Gruagagh nodded. "It will be in Gyre the Elder's
Keep.''

"Where's that?"

"I'll show you.''

He tugged a fat leather shoulder bag from under the windowseat and took out a roll of parchment that he laid out
between them. A startled "Oh" escaped Jacky as she bent
over it. The map was of Ottawa, but all the names were
changed. Parliament Hill was the Laird's Manor and Court.
The Market area was the Easting Fair. The Glebe became
Cockle Tom's Garve.

"This shows Kinrowan," the Gruagagh said. "Kinrowan
proper—the Laird's Seat. And this is the countryside, showing the boundaries of our realm.''

Everything was familiar, but foreign at the same time. The
shapes of the streets and the placements of surrounding vil-
lages and towns were all as they should be, but reading the
names Jacky felt as though she'd stepped through Alice's
looking glass, and everything had been turned around.

"It's all different," she said.

"Just the names. We have our own. And the Court of Kinrowan is not the only Seelie Court either.'' He pointed to the
area north of the Ottawa River where the Gatineau Hills began. "This is the Laird of Dunlogan's realm.'' Now he pulled
out a second map and the finger moved down it, from Kinrowan towards Kingston. "And this is Kenrose. But there are
gaps, you see. Here and here.'' He pointed out shaded areas
between the various faerie realms.

"These are the Borderlands where the fiaina sidhe dwell—
the wild faerie that have no allegiance to either Court. But
because the fiaina take no side, the Unseelie Court can host
against us in the Borderlands—unopposed.'' He pointed to
Winchester. "Here is a place where the Host has driven out

a Laird's Court, taking it for their own. Such places grow almost daily now.

"This map's not so new now and some of the borders have changed, for as Gyre the Elder's people grow in strength, our own borders shrink. There was a time, Jacky, when you wouldn't see a bogan though you walked from the High Dales of Dunlogan down to Avon Dhu." He pointed to the St. Lawrence Seaway as he spoke. "But now . . . now Gyre the Younger stands outside my Tower, penning me in, and sluagh whisper on the winds that creep between the boards."

"Can't these other Lairds help you?" Jacky asked.

The Gruagagh shook his head. "They're as bad off as we are—if not worse."

"What about these wild faerie?"

"The fiaina are impossible to gather under one banner. They are a solitary folk and won't see the danger until it's too late. Since the Host has made no move against them to date, they appear content to remain uninvolved. It's an evil time, Jacky Rowan, and it's not getting any better."

She pointed to the first map. "It says 'The Gruagagh's Tower' here," she said, indicating the house they were in. On the map, Belmont Avenue had become Auch Ward Way. "Why does it say Tower? This is just a house."

"In the homeland, the gruagaghs all had Towers," he explained. "We're a folk that stick hard to tradition, so that even if the building's not a tower, we'll call it one all the same."

"Here's Tamson House," Jacky said, still poring over the map. She glanced up at him. "It's called that in our world as well."

The Gruagagh nodded. "That is an old magic place—a doorway to the Otherworlds of the spirits who were here before we came."

Well, there was certainly something odd about the block-long building, Jacky thought. It had always fascinated her when she walked by—especially the towers—but she'd never been inside.

"Where is Gyre the Elder's Keep?" she asked.

The Gruagagh opened the second map again and showed her. She had to think for a moment before she could find the proper name for the place—at least the name she knew it by.

"That's near Calabogie," she said at last. It was an hour west of Ottawa and she'd had a picnic at a friend's cottage near there just this summer. "But I don't remember seeing anything that looked even vaguely like a Keep." Then she smiled. "But it's not a Keep, is it? You just call it that."

The Gruagagh nodded. "The Giants' Keep is a cave—a well-guarded cave, Jacky. You'll find it hard to get near to it, little say inside, even with a hob skillyman's stitcheries to help you."

"But I have to try, don't I?"

The Gruagagh nodded again. "I suppose you must."

"If I get the Horn, will you help me call the Wild Hunt? We can set it on the giants and see how much *they* like it."

"I can't help you," the Gruagagh said. "And you must not return here. They have marked you now. Once in and out of my Tower and they may let you go—or just follow and watch, to see who and what you are. Twice in and out, and they'll know you for an enemy and they will kill you."

"Why can't they get into this house?"

"Because 'this house' is my Tower—a gruagagh's Tower—and I use all my diminishing powers to keep the Host at bay. To protect the Laird's heart, to protect the realm. It and the Laird's Court are the only safe havens in all of Kinrowan now. The only other safety is to tread softly so that they don't see you."

"That's why the hob was running across the park last night," Jacky said. "He would've been safe if he'd reached this place. And that's why you didn't go out to help him— you couldn't."

"Just as I won't be able to help you once you leave here," the Gruagagh said. "You can go back to your old life, Jacky Rowan, and no one will think ill of you, for this isn't your war, no matter what your name. But if you do bring the Laird's daughter back safe, you can ask anything of me, and it will be yours."

"I . . . I don't want anything. I just want to help."

"You're a brave lass, Jacky."

She smiled quickly, pushing down the panic that was demanding to be heard. She was trying to be brave, though she didn't really know why.

"If you do reach the Keep," the Gruagagh continued,

"you will still have to find the Horn. It won't be lying in plain sight, nor will Gyre the Elder keep it with him. He can use it, but it makes him uneasy, so it will be hidden."

"How do I find it then?"

"By your name."

"That doesn't tell me anything."

"Rowan," the Gruagagh said. "It will be marked by the berries of the rowan. No matter what Gyre the Elder has disguised it as, you'll know it by the berries. Like your name: Berryred. Which makes us closer kin than you think."

Jacky nodded. He'd told her earlier. His bardic name, Dearg, meant red.

"Bhruic," she said. "What's the name—the speaking name—of the Laird's daughter?"

"Lorana."

His features grew bleak and grim as he spoke her name. For a long moment silence lay between them until at last Jacky stirred.

"I'd better be going," she said.

The Gruagagh nodded. He rolled up the maps and returned them to their storage place, then rummaged about in the pack for a moment or two. When he found what he was looking for, he took Jacky's hand and pressed a small brooch into it. It was made of silver and took the shape of a tiny staff, crossed by a sprig of berries. Rowan berries, she knew. And the staff would be rowan, too.

"Take this," he said.

"What . . . what does it do?"

"Do?" The Gruagagh smiled. "It doesn't do anything. It's just to remind you of me—it's my way of thanking you for trying what my own people won't dare."

It was all those magic stitcheries that Finn had put into her jacket and sneakers, Jacky realized. They made her think that anything she got from faerie would . . . do something.

"I'm sorry," she said. "I didn't mean—"

"I know."

The Gruagagh arose and she stood quickly with him.

"Don't go searching out the Giants' Keep straightaway," he warned her. "The Host will be watching you to see what you do and if you set off immediately, your quest will be doomed before you even start. Go back to your own life for a day or two. Let the Host grow weary of your routine. And then go.

"Wear your hob coat—it will hide you from most eyes at night, if not so well by day. The cap will serve you well, too. It allows you more than sight. Wearing it is what lets you accept more easily all these new things you've seen these past few nights."

He took the brooch from her hand and pinned it to her jacket.

"How come I could see you the other night?" Jacky asked. "You and the hob and the riders and everything?"

The Gruagagh shrugged. "Sometimes your people stray into our realm. Grief will bring you—or strong drink. A sudden shock."

Jacky blushed thinking of strong drink. The Gruagagh turned and extinguished the candle by simply looking at it. Jacky shivered in the darkness, the reality of it all coming home again. There was a rider outside, watching, waiting. And a Big Man. . . .

The Gruagagh opened the door and stepped to one side. "Luck be with you, Jacky Rowan."

Jacky peered out into the shadows of the back yard and hesitated. Then she frowned at herself. She stole a glance at the Gruagagh and impulsively stood on her tiptoes to give him a quick kiss, then was out the door.

The Gruagagh watched her go, startled. He lifted a finger to his lips and the shadows in his eyes deepened. If duty didn't bind him, he thought, then sighed. But duty did. And so Lorana was captured or worse, and this Jacky Rowan was going out to tilt with giants, and he was trapped, bound to his duty. By his oath. By the need of the realm.

"Luck," he said again softly and closed the door.

"Finn?" Jacky whispered at the foot of the garden.

She started to look up into his tree, but then she saw that the rider on the far side of the park was no longer alone. She froze against the cedar hedge, her voice caught in her throat. There were two of them now. She bit at her lip. Would they go away if she took off her redcap? Or would they still be there, invisible? She glanced back at the Gruagagh's Tower, wishing she hadn't left its safety.

"Finn?" she whispered again and shot a look up his tree. She saw the hob sitting there, clutching the trunk. He turned to look down at her, a finger to his lips. Jacky followed his gaze and saw that he wasn't looking at the riders, but at the Big Man.

Gyre the Younger. An eighteen foot high giant. Here in the middle of Windsor Park. He shouldn't exist, but he did. And he was turning to look in their direction.

Frightened in earnest now, all Jacky could do was crouch by the hedge. She felt the ground tremble slightly as the giant lifted one foot, put it down, lifted the other, turned. Then he started across the park towards her.

CHAPTER
5

He was big, this giant. Bigger than any creature Jacky had ever seen. His head alone was more than two feet high, almost a foot and a half wide. Legs, three yards long, supported the enormous bulk of his torso and carried him across the park. He was going to be right on top of her in moments and she didn't know what to do. She was too petrified with fear to do more than shake where she was crouched. Her fingers plucked nervously at the hem of her jacket and she chewed furiously on her lower lip.

Run, she told herself. Get up and run, you fool. Find some place too small for him to follow. Be a fieldmouse to his cat and find some hiding place to burrow into.

But she couldn't move. Then Finn dropped from his tree with a rustle of leaves and was crouching beside her.

"I'll lead him off," he whispered urgently. "He doesn't quite know what's here, I'm thinking, so if he sees me run off, he'll give chase to me. The stitcheries in your coat will keep you hidden so long as you *don't move*!"

"B-but . . . what about you . . . ?

"He won't catch me. Only the Hunt could catch me, but they won't follow. There's only two of them. They need their full ranks for a proper hunt."

"But—"

"Stay!" His gaze fell on the Gruagagh's brooch and he frowned, then quickly shrugged. "I'll find you," he added.

"As quick as I've lost him, I'll find you. Stay till he gives chase, then go as quick as you can to a safe place."

The only safe place Jacky could think of was the Gruagagh's Tower behind them. But before she could say anything, the giant was looming over them.

"Hey-aha!" Finn cried at the top of his lungs. "Laird, but you're an ugly creature, Gyre the Younger!"

And then he was off with the same speed that had astonished Jacky earlier. She pressed against the ground, close to the hedge, trying to make as small a target of herself as she could. She expected to feel those great big hands lifting her, squeezing the life from her.

The ground trembled under the giant's tread, like an echo of the shivers that fear sent through her. She peeped open an eye to see the giant turning and heading in the direction that Finn had taken. Relief went through her for one long blissful moment, then she thought of Finn with that monstrous man on his heels. If the giant ever caught hold of him . . . She shuddered.

She stayed hidden by the hedge until the rumble of the giant's footsteps faded before slowly getting to her feet. Her bones were all watery, but she knew she had to go now, or she'd never get away at all. She glanced at the Gruagagh's Tower, but Bhruic wasn't at the window. A second glance went across the park to where the two riders sat on their gleaming machines. Then she gathered the tattered remnants of her courage and crept away, following the hedge to the back yard of one of the neighbouring houses and from there onto Belmont Avenue.

Just as she was congratulating herself on her escape, the sound of a big Harley starting up came from the direction of the park. She reminded herself that the Hunt needed its full ranks to be dangerous, but that didn't do much to ease her fear. For someone like her, they probably didn't need more than one of the riders.

She took to her heels and ran, the hob stitcheries in her sneakers lending her speed that she could never have managed on her own. From the park, the sound of the motorcycle grew louder.

Finn led the giant for a merry chase, up streets and down the back alleys where the earlier residents of the cities had once kept their horses and buggies. He made sure to always stay just in sight of his monstrous pursuer so that the giant wouldn't give up the chase until Jacky had had time to make good her escape.

Gyre the Younger moved more quickly than one might have supposed from his initial lumbering pace across the park. He took steps of three yards or more at a time, and it was only the speedy stitcheries in the hob's own brown leather shoes that kept Finn ahead. Where the hob darted between parked cars, Gyre the Younger stepped over them. Where Finn squeezed through fences and dove under hedges, the looming giant continued to merely step over each obstruction.

They passed a couple, out for a late night stroll with their dog. Neither human noticed the faerie, but the hackles on their pet rose as Finn brushed by. The dog began to growl and bark after the fleeing hob, but then the giant was there and it whined, trying to hide between the legs of its master.

"Damn dog," the man said. "I don't know what's gotten into him."

Finn never heard the woman's response. He was already out of earshot, barely dodging a car on Riverdale. The driver never saw him, invisible as the hob was, but Finn gave him a curse anyway as he ran on. The car had come too close for comfort. Behind him, Gyre the Younger gave a booming laugh.

That was enough for Finn. He judged that he'd given Jacky enough time to make her own escape, so he put on a new burst of speed, finally losing the giant in the trees up behind Pearly Hospital. He stood and listened to the night, but it was quiet now. When he was sure that the giant had given up, Finn made his way to the convenient back steps of a house and sat down. There he let loose the string of curses that he hadn't had the breath to mouth earlier.

"Damn him, and damn his brother, and damn all his kin," he finished up with. "May he lose his head in a bogan's arse, looking for nits. May he feed on sores. May he fall asleep and let me stitch his mouth and nose fast shut, and then I'll watch him choke, and I'll smile, oh yes. Won't I just grin? Oh, damn!"

It was not so long ago that only the Laird's folk held Kinrowan and the Host kept to its own reaches. He could still remember when it was safe to have a gathery-up of hobs anywhere you pleased, and never have to worry about bogans or the restless dead. But times had changed, and were still changing, and none for the better.

"Oh, damn," he muttered again, scowling at his feet.

Gyre the Younger had this hob's smell, yes he did. And if he wanted, he could set the Hunt on him—just like he'd done to poor old Redfairn Tom. Finn's anger turned to sorrow, thinking of his cousin, and then he remembered Jacky. He sighed and rose silently to his feet. He supposed he had better fetch her.

What he'd told her was true: he wouldn't let anyone fall into the clutches of the Host. Not if he could help it. But that didn't explain why he'd told her all that he had or why he'd gifted her with stitcheries. That was more than just help, but it had seemed right at the time. Just as his leading the giant away from her had been, and going to fetch her now was. They, too, seemed like things that must be done. It was poor Tom's cap, he supposed. That had made him feel kindly to her at first. And then there was her name.

He set off at a grumbling walk, hoping she'd had the good common sense to head off for a safe place once he'd led Gyre the Younger away. She was an odd sort of a girl, he thought. Brave and frightened all at the same time. Fey as his own kin sometimes, but then so bloody mortal it made him wonder that a stitchery spell would even work for her. Oh, but it took all sorts, now didn't it?

He didn't wonder too much about what had happened between her and the Gruagagh in the Gruagagh's Tower—at least not until he was on Auch Ward Way, with the Tower in front of him, and no sign of her anywhere around. He should have been able to trace the trail of his own stitcheries—a trail not one of the Host would sense, though perhaps the Hunt could. The Hunt followed the smell of your soul.

It was as he cast up and down the street, then finally snuck into the neighbouring back yards to assure himself that she wasn't still huddled by the hedge, that he realized what had happened.

"What game's he playing now?" he muttered.

For he remembered the Gruagagh's brooch he'd seen

pinned to her jacket and knew that it was some spell of the Gruagagh's that was stopping him from following the lingering trail of his own stitcheries. He paused in the middle of the street, scowling through his beard. He debated going back to his lookout tree by the Gruagagh's Tower, but he knew that the Big Man would be watching it very closely now.

So he needed a new tree to perch in—and what? Should he follow the girl, or leave her to her own devices? He was partly responsible for whatever she was up to, that much was certain. He'd given her stitcheries and pointed the way to the Gruagagh's door. He wondered if the Gruagagh had told her where the Horn was and if she truly meant to go after it. Only what if it had been the Gruagagh who had set that giant after her?

"Oh, I don't like thinking," he told the empty street.

Cloaked with the stitcheries sewn into his own coat, he crept into the back yard of a house a few doors down from the Gruagagh's Tower and stole a quick peek out across the park. When he saw just the one rider on his Harley and the giant still gone, he knew trouble was brewing. The giant would be fetching his kin—or the Horn to call up the Hunt— while the missing rider would be following Jacky.

He had to find her first. He was the one who had filled her head with all that nonsense about asking the Gruagagh for help and rescuing the Laird's daughter. Scowling at the dark shadow of the Gruagagh's Tower, he made his way back to the street. Deciding to find her was one thing, he realized once he stood there. Only where did he begin?

"Oh, damn," he muttered.

Choosing a direction at random, he set off. But Jacky had gone the other way.

As the sound of the Harley grew louder, Jacky cut across a lawn, scrambled over a fence to run alongside the house and through its back yard. At the foot of the yard, she squeezed through a hedge and paused to get her bearings.

At least he won't be able to follow me through all that, she thought, looking back the way she'd come.

She was in between Fentiman and Belmont now. Still too far from her apartment on Ossington. Go to a safe place, Finn had told her—oh, don't let the giant have caught him! But what was a safe place? Some place with people. A restaurant or bar.

Oh, think! she told herself.

She could hear the biker on Belmont now. The nearest restaurants were on Bank Street, but that was too far for her to go right now. There were too many streets to cross—open spaces where the biker could spot her. Then she thought of Kate. Kate lived just up on Sunnyside. Was she back from her mother's yet? Would going there put Kate in danger, too?

The Harley was idling on the street in front of the house now, making it too hard to think. She could imagine the rider putting his machine on its kickstand, coming around back of the house to get her . . .

She bolted towards Fentiman, tore the leg of her jeans going over a low fence, and sprawled across the lawn, but was up and racing for the open street as fast as her legs could carry her. She heard the Harley roar on Belmont behind her. The dryness had returned to her throat and her pulse drummed. Crossing the street, she plunged down the first laneway she came to. The biker came around the corner at the same time, his headlight like a searching eye. Had he seen her?

Another back yard, another fence, and then she was on Brighton, just one block away from Kate's street. Again the Harley appeared around the corner, this time well before she was out of sight. The biker started down the street, catching her in his headlight as she dashed for the next driveway.

The sound of the bike was like growling thunder in her ears. She panted for breath as she ran. Adrenaline and Finn's stitcheries got her to the end of the lane before the biker reached it. She dodged around the garage, through another yard. Now she could see Sunnyside through the gaps in the houses in front of her. Again she had to pause to get her bearings. Kate's apartment was a ground floor—on this side of the street, thank God!—and it was—

She picked her direction and started off through the back yards, heedless of flowerbeds and small vegetable patches, hauling herself over fences. One back yard, another. A third. The roar of the Harley was a constant drone in her ears. It made her teeth shake. The bike was on Sunnyside now, pacing her. Any moment she expected it to roar down a driveway and cut her off. But then Kate's back door was in front of her and she was up the stairs and hammering on it.

Please be home, oh, *please* be home.

The Harley was idling on the street in front of the house. The slower rev of its engine was somehow more frightening to her than the sound of it coming down the street after her. She pressed her cheek against the door, still knocking on it. A light went on over the door, half-blinding her. When the door itself opened inwards, she lost her balance.

"Who the hell—" Kate began.

Jacky caught her balance and leaned against the doorjamb. She looked into her friend's angry face, saw the anger drawing away to be replaced by shock.

"It . . . it's just me," she said. "Jacky." But then she realized what she must look like, with the redcap on her head and her cornstubble hair sticking out from underneath it like a scarecrow's straw, with her clothes torn and her face and hands smudged with dirt.

"My God," Kate said. "Jacky, what's happened?"

Her friend's voice was suddenly loud in Jacky's ears—very loud—and then she realized that she couldn't hear the roar of the biker's Harley anymore. He must have killed the engine on his machine.

"I . . . I've been having a weird night since you left my place," she said.

"No kidding? You look like something the cat dragged in. And where'd you get this?"

Kate plucked the cap from Jacky's head. Jacky blinked, vertigo hitting her hard. When the world settled down once more, it wasn't such a bright place anymore. It was as though taking off the cap had drained something from it—a certain vitality, an inner glow that was now washed away. She tried to smile at Kate, but she was having trouble just leaning against the doorjamb.

"Can I come in?" she asked.

Kate took her by the arm and led her inside, shutting the door on the night.

CHAPTER
6

If she could share her current craziness with anyone, Jacky thought, it would be Kate, but what had been happening lately seemed too off the wall to share even with her, best friend or not. So Jacky told her nothing about hobs or gruagaghs, stitcheries, giants or the Wild Hunt. Instead she described being chased by a biker, and how she hoped that she hadn't brought any trouble with her by knocking on Kate's door.

"Creepy," Kate said when she was done.

"Yeah, but if he's still hanging around. . . ."

"Oh, I wouldn't worry about that. He's had his fun. He's probably back at some bar with the rest of his asshole friends, having a good yuk about it."

If he wasn't gathering up the rest of the Hunt, Jacky thought uncomfortably.

Kate turned from the kitchen counter where she was making some tea. "Hungry?" she asked.

"No—yes. I'm starving."

"I've got cake—or I could make you a sandwich."

"I'll take the cake."

Kate grinned. "I kind of thought you would."

Jacky stuck out her tongue and relaxed in her chair. The effects of her latest encounter with faerie were beginning to wear off a little now as she sat in the familiar comfort of her friend's kitchen. The table she was sitting at was in a little breakfast nook that jutted out from the rest of the house into

the back yard, with windows on three sides. There were
enough plants hanging in there to start a jungle, together with
various and sundry postcards that were tacked to the window
frames and little odds and ends that were perched wherever
there was a spot for them.

Jacky watched Kate bustle about getting tea mugs, pouring
the water into the kettle, cutting a generous slice of nutcake
for each of them. If there was one thing that Kate was mad
about, it was nuts of every size, shape and description which,
considering her surname Hazel, left her open to a great deal
of teasing.

Jacky knew that she should get up and wash her hands and
face, but she just didn't have the energy. It was so much
better just lolling here in the nook, and then Kate was loading
up the table and, well, Jacky thought, it would be rude to get
up just when Kate was sitting down.

The tea was hot and perfect. The cake was homemade,
hazelnut—which brought a suitable comment from Jacky as
she tasted it—and delicious.

"Maybe," Kate said in reply, with her chin propped up
on her hands as she studied Jacky's hair, "we could hire you
out as a sort of walking broom." She plucked the redcap
from the floor where it had fallen. "And where did you get
this?"

"I found it."

"I can believe it. I just didn't think you were the sort to
go through dustbins." She scrunched up her face and lowered
her voice. "It's a dirty job, but somebody's got to do it."

Jacky snatched the hat back from her, then sat turning it
over in her hand.

"Hey," Kate said. "I was just teasing."

"I know."

Jacky looked inside the cap and traced the intricate stitches
she found there with her finger. Hob stitcheries, she thought.
The dead hob who had owned it flashed in her mind . . . the
angle of his neck as he lay on the ground, the sightless eyes.
And then she thought of Finn, leading off the giant . . . She
glanced at Kate.

"Do you believe in . . . in faeries?" she asked.

"Faeries as in gay, or faeries as in Tinkerbell?"

"As in Tinkerbell—but not all cutesy like that. More like

faerie as in the realm of Faerie, with gnomes and wizards and giants and that sort of thing.''

"Seriously?''

"Seriously.''

Kate shook her head. " 'Fraid not. Are you doing a survey?''

"No. What about ghosts? You know, vampires and the walking dead and spooks that come out at night?''

"Well, I don't know about *ze* Count and his friends, but ghosts . . . maybe ghosts.''

"Really?''

Kate sighed and poured them both some more tea. "Well, not *really*. But sometimes when I'm alone at night and the house's creaking—you know. You get that feeling. Would *you* stay overnight in a graveyard?''

"I suppose not.''

And there it was, Jacky thought. The first person she asked confirmed what Finn had told her. People believed in the darker creatures of Faerie, in ghosts and the undead, far more readily than they did in gnomes and the like. She was sure that if she asked anybody she knew, they'd come up with pretty much the same answer as Kate had given her.

"What's with all this talk about spooks?'' Kate asked. "Have you been reading Stephen King again?''

"I wish I was just reading about it.''

"What?''

Jacky frowned. "Nothing,'' she said.

"Come on, Jacky. I know something's bothering you.'' She looked at Jacky, then shook her head. "God, what am I saying? First Will walks all over you, and then some lunatic on a motorcycle chases you all around Ottawa South. I wouldn't exactly be jumping for joy either. This guy didn't hurt you, did he?''

"No. But what if I told you I'd seen a gnome tonight?''

"I'd say 'That's nice.' ''

"No, seriously.''

"I am being serious—it's you that's not making any sense.''

"What if I could prove it?''

Kate laughed. "Please don't pull out some clipping from the *National Enquirer*.''

"No. I mean, what if I could show you what I meant?''

"You're really serious?"

Jacky nodded.

"Oh, jeez. Now you're scaring me."

"Look," Jacky said. "This biker that was chasing me—"

"He was a gnome? Hell's Gnomes? Come *on*."

"No. He's not a gnome. He's a part of some kind of Wild Hunt. Remember in Caitlin Midhir's book *Yarthkin*, when those riders are chasing the girl and one of them's got these big antlers? It's like that. Except they're riding motorcycles."

"Antlered men riding motorcycles?"

"I didn't say he had antlers," Jacky said a little crossly.

Kate held up a hand. "Time out. This is getting too weird for me, Jacky. And it's scaring me because it's not like you at all."

"Is it because you've never seen anything like it before?"

"Well, that's good for starters."

"Well, you've never been to Japan before either. How do you know *it* exists?"

"I've seen pictures. I know people who've been there. I saw it in a movie."

"Well, I saw *Gremlins*, but that doesn't mean those little things are real. But this rider is, Kate. And I can prove it."

Kate sighed. "Okay. For the sake of argument, prove it."

"We have to go to the front of the house," Jacky said standing up.

As she led the way, the redcap dangling from her hand, she was of two minds. On the one hand she wanted to prove to Kate that what she'd been experiencing was real, just to have someone else who could see it, someone to be there to tell her that she wasn't going crazy. Because that was scary. But on the other hand, if the rider was there, that was even scarier.

She didn't know what she was hoping for, but by then they'd reached the living room. Standing by the front window, they looked out at the street. There was no one there. Just some parked cars. A cat was lying on the hood of one— the engine was probably still warm and it was stealing what heat it could before the metal cooled down.

"So now what happens?" Kate asked, peering up and down the street.

"You don't see anything out there, right?"

"Right. So therefore your gnomes are real?"

"Kate!"

"Okay, okay. Tell me what to do. Do I stand on one leg and squint out of the corner of my eye, or . . ." She let her voice trail off at Jacky's frown.

"Just don't do anything for a moment," Jacky said. Then she put on the redcap, bracing herself for the sense of vertigo that was going to come.

It wasn't so bad this time—more like a subtle shifting underfoot—and then a gauze seemed to have dropped from her eyes so that she could see everything clearly again. The redcap alone should prove it, she thought, but looking out the window she saw him, the chrome of his machine gleaming in the streetlights, the black leather swallowing light, the featureless shadow under his visor. She stared for a long moment, shivering, then stepped back.

"Jacky," Kate began worriedly.

Jacky shook her head and took off the redcap. She kept her balance by holding on to the windowsill, then handed the cap to Kate.

"Put it on and look out the window," she said. "Down there towards the house where that guy was working on his car almost every day last summer."

Kate stepped closer to the window and looked.

"Put the cap on," Jacky said.

Kate turned. "But there's nothing there."

"Please?"

"Okay, okay."

She put the redcap on and Jacky stepped in close to steady her as she swayed dizzily.

"My God," Kate said softly. "There *is* someone out there." She turned from the window. "We've got to call the cops . . ." Her voice faded as she looked at Jacky.

"What's the matter?" Jacky asked.

"I don't know. You look different all of a sudden. It's like I can see you better or something."

Jacky nodded. "Look at the biker again," she said. "Is he still there?" she added, once Kate was looking in the right direction.

When Kate nodded, Jacky pulled the cap from her head and then steadied her again. Kate swayed, looked out the window, then back at Jacky. Without saying anything, she moved slowly to a chair and sat down.

"It's a trick, right?" she said when she was sitting down.

Jacky shook her head. "No. It's real. The cap lets you see into Faerie."

"Faerie," Kate repeated numbly. "Now they're going to take both of us away in nice little white jackets."

"We're *not* crazy," Jacky said.

Kate didn't say anything for a long moment. Then she asked, "Where did you get that . . . that cap?"

"From a gnome."

"From a . . . God, I'm sorry I asked."

Jacky started to frown, but then she saw that it was just Kate's way of dealing with it.

"Let's go have some more tea," she said, "and I'll tell you all about it."

Kate pushed herself up, using the arms of the chair for leverage, and followed her into the kitchen.

"The floor's yours," she said.

Kate tended to frown when she concentrated on something. By the time Jacky was finished her story, her forehead was a grid of lines.

"You shouldn't do that," Jacky said.

Kate looked at her. "Do what?"

"Scrunch up your face like that. My mother used to say when I was pulling a face, that if I didn't watch out, the wind would change and leave me looking like that forever."

"Or until the wind changed again," Kate added.

She put her index fingers in either side of her mouth and pulled it open in a gaping grin, then rolled her eyes. Jacky burst into laughter.

"Of course," Kate said when they'd both caught their breath, "I suppose we've got to take all that shit seriously now, don't we? Black cats and walking under ladders—the whole kit and kaboodle."

"Oh, I don't know," Jacky replied. "But . . . you *do* believe me now, don't you?"

Kate looked at the redcap, then at her friend's face. "Yeah," she said slowly. "I guess I do. And now—like I said before. What happens? You're not really going to this Giants' Castle to look for the Horn, are you?''

''I have to.''

''Why?''

''I don't know. Because of Bhruic and Finn, I suppose. Because no one else will and this is finally something I can do that'll have meaning.''

Kate shook her head. ''Will was full of it and you know it. What the hell kind of meaning do you call his way of living? I still don't know what you ever saw in him.''

''Well, he had nice buns.''

''Woman does not live by buns alone.''

Jacky smiled.

''So how are you getting out there?'' Kate asked.

''I hadn't really thought about it. By bus, I suppose. Do you think a bus goes out there?''

''We could take Judith.'' Judith was Kate's Volkswagen Beetle that had surprisingly survived God knew how many Ottawa winters.

Jacky shook her head. ''No way.''

''Why? You don't think she'd make it out there?''

''It's not that. I don't want you to come. This is something I've got to do, but I'm not going to drag you into it.''

''Then why did you tell me about it? Why point out that geek on his bike to me?''

Jacky sighed. ''I just wanted somebody else to know. I wanted to see if somebody else could see him too. So that I wouldn't have to keep wondering if I was just crazy, you know?''

''Well, you are crazy, but that's got nothing to do with this. I'm going, and that's final. A woman's got to do what a woman's got to do and all that.''

''But it's not your problem.''

''It wasn't yours either, Jacky. But you've made it yours— just like I'm making it mine.''

''I couldn't stand it if something happened to you.''

''Hey, I'm not all that big on sitting around her wondering if I'll ever see you again either, you know. We're pals, right? So what do pals do but stick up for each other? I'm going. If you don't want to come with me in Judith, then I'll just meet you there.''

"But you didn't see them kill that little hob, Kate. And the giant—he's *so* big."

"We'll be like that little tailor in the fairy tale—remember? 'Seven with one blow.' No! I'll be the valiant tailor. And you . . . you'll be Jack the Giant-Killer."

"It's not funny, Kate. And I don't want to kill anybody."

Kate reached out to hold Jacky's hand. She gave it a squeeze. "I know, Jacky. I'm scared too. I'm just shooting off my mouth so that I don't have to think about it. You're sleeping here tonight, aren't you?" When Jacky nodded, she added, "Well, then let's hit the sack, okay?"

"Okay."

Jacky lay awake for a long time after she went to bed. She kept wanting to get up to make sure that the biker hadn't come any closer to the house, that the rest of the Hunt hadn't joined him. She worried about Finn, and about Kate coming with her to the Giants' Keep, and was of half a mind to sneak out right now, but she knew it was too late. Kate would just drive out to Calabogie herself and be sitting there waiting for her.

She listened to the wind outside her window. It was making a funny sound—almost breathing. She thought of what Bhruic had told her, about how he heard the whispery voices of the sluagh, the restless dead, on the winds at night.

She turned her head so that she could see the window from where she lay. When she started to imagine that she could see faces pressing against the panes—horrible faces, all bloated like drowned corpses—she slipped from under the covers and went into Kate's bedroom. Kate stirred as Jacky crept into her bed, but she didn't wake.

Listening carefully now, all Jacky could hear was the sound of their own breathing, nothing more. She felt a little stupid for getting spooked—and what did that say about how she'd do when it came to their expedition to the Giants' Keep?— but foolish or not, she was staying right where she was and she wasn't going to budge until it was morning.

CHAPTER
7

The rumour touched all of Faerie that night: there was a new hope in the Seelie Court—a small one, true, but a hope all the same—and she meant to free the Laird's daughter and would too, except that if the hogans didn't get to her, then surely the Wild Hunt would. But whether she was doomed or not, the rumour of her ran from the heart of Kinrowan to the Borderlands. It was heard by the fiaina sidhe in their solitary haunts, and by the Seelie Court and the Host alike.

Hidden in a tree from which he could view both Manswater and Underbridge (the Rideau Canal and Lansdowne Bridge, respectively) with equal ease, Dunrobin Finn listened to the rumours, listened hard to hear if the Unseelie Court was looking for a hob skillyman as well. It wasn't, not so that he heard, but he frowned all the same.

"Now she's done it," he muttered to himself. "She won't get five feet from whatever hidey-hole she's found, little say recover the Laird's daughter now—not with half the Host looking for her tonight. And the Hunt . . ."

He pursed his lips and studied the sky. The night was draining quickly into morning. Too late for the Hunt to ride tonight perhaps, but it would be out tomorrow night, and then Jacky Rowan would know what it meant to be afraid.

"And they'll be looking for her today," he added aloud. "Those that can abide the light of day."

He could see the troll who lived in Underbridge stirring,

sifting through the rubbish he called his treasure. Looking for a sword, Finn thought. Looking for something with which to cut himself a piece of Jacky Rowan before he took what was left of her to Gyre the Elder.

"Oh, Jacky Rowan. You'd better learn or steal a greatspell damn quick if you want to live out the day."

Finn frowned again, fingers plucking nervously at his beard. Oh, she was in trouble, deep trouble, there was no doubt about that, and he'd as much as thrown her to the wolves himself. If he'd just left well enough alone. Snatched Tom's cap from her, maybe. Never told her about the Gruagagh, surely. Minded his own business like a good hob couldn't.

"And that's the trick, isn't it?" he said to the night. "To be a good hob, you've got to stick your nose into a place or two and play your tricks, or what are you? Not a hob, that's for damn sure."

In Underbridge, the troll had found a rusty old sword and was now rubbing it on the big stone supports of the bridge. The grinding noise was loud coming across the water of the canal and it set Finn's teeth on edge.

And they'll all be doing that, he thought. Sharpening their weapons—those that have weapons. He shivered, remembering all the sluagh he'd seen go by tonight. A troll's stupid face, with its crooked teeth and mismatched eyes, nose like a big bird's beak—that was nothing like the faces of the restless dead. They had a drowned look about them—pale and bloated.

From across the canal, the troll's grinding continued. Finn scurried down his tree at last, mind made up. He was looking for Jacky Rowan, so it was best he got back to it. Best he found her, before something else did.

"And that's one thing for rumours," he said as he set off at a quick run, south and east. "They tell you where to go."

Like following the thread of one of his own hob stitcheries, he chased the threads of the rumors. They led him through Cockle Tom's Garve, back and forth across the Manswater, then down into Crowdie Wort's Bally, where he'd first met and then lost Jacky earlier that night. Here the rumours were too thick, the threads twisting in and out of each other, for him to locate exactly where she was.

"But she's here," he said as he found a perch in a comfortable old oak tree on Killbrodie Way, which is the faerie name for Sunnyside Avenue. "And close, too. I'll bide a bit, now won't I, Mistress Oak, snug in your arms. Then we'll see what the morning brings."

Three blocks east, the Big Man's sluagh were gathered around Kate Hazel's house, peering through windows, looking for a way in. But the latches were all latched, the doors locked, and there was no one awake that they could trick into letting them in. Then the night finally drained away and they returned to their marshes, the bogans to their sewer dens, the trolls to their bridges.

Dunrobin Finn lay fast asleep in the arms of a Mother Oak, and the black rider kicked his Harley into life outside Kate Hazel's house. The chopper coughed loudly in the still street, a sound heard only in Faerie, and pulled away from the curb.

Another night was only hours away and he could be patient. He would have his brothers with him then. Let the hope of the Laird's folk sleep for now, for tonight the full Hunt would ride and there would be no escape. Not any at all.

The Gruagagh of Kinrowan watched the sun come up, pinking the eastern skies. For long silent moments he stared out the window of his house, that in Faerie was his Tower, then he turned at last from the view and sighed. The rumours had touched him as well—from the swollen lips of the sluagh, on the airy voices of those gnomes that rode the wind.

A hope? he asked the silent room. He remembered too well the power of the Unseelie Court.

That girl, he thought. She had the name—both Rowan and Jack—so there was more than luck in her arrival at the Tower tonight. But the task was hard. She would need help and friends, and with the Host's ranks swelling more every day, where would she find either?

Better a small hope than none at all, the rumouring tongues of the wind gnomes whispered outside the Tower.

Unhappily, the Gruagagh returned to the window to watch the sunlight wash Learg Green with her light. The park glistened. The skies were a brilliant blue. But there was misfortune in the air. The Gruagagh could taste it. Like Finn, he knew he had pushed Jacky into danger, but unlike the hob, he couldn't follow after to try to help. The Tower protected him, but it kept him a prisoner as well. He could only listen to the gossip on the wind and wonder at the fate of the hope of Kinrowan.

CHAPTER
8

When Jacky woke, the bed beside her was empty. She had time for one blind moment of panic, then she saw the note pinned to the pillow beside her, and relaxed. Stilling the thunder of her pulse, she pulled the note free. It said, in Kate's familiar scrawl that passed for her handwriting:

> Wimped out, didja? Well, don't
> panic. Mother Kate's just gone
> to the store to get us some goodies.
> Back soon.
>   K.

Jacky grinned. She supposed she'd never hear the end of this. But last night, she was sure there'd been something at the window, peering in. Something that called to her, to open wide the windows . . . Right now, all that made its way through the panes was a wash of sunshine.

Slipping out of bed, Jacky padded to the bathroom, wearing the oversized T-shirt that she'd borrowed last night to serve as a nightie. By the time she was dressed and sitting in the kitchen, frowning over the long tear in her jeans, Kate was back and making them both a breakfast of sausages and pancakes. Two mugs of coffee steamed on the table in the breakfast nook.

"So, when are we going?" Kate asked. She drifted over

to the table to take a sip of her coffee before returning to the stove to fuss with their breakfast.

"I can't even believe it's real anymore," Jacky said.

"Then why'd you crawl into bed with me last night?" Kate asked. "Or have you just given up on men?"

Jacky blushed. "No. It's just . . ."

"I know." Kate concentrated on pouring a new batch of batter without spilling any of it over the sides of the frying pan into the burner. While she was waiting for airholes to appear on the tops of the pancakes so that she could flip them, she turned back to look at Jacky. "But what are we going to do?"

Jacky ran a hand through the stubble of her hair. "I thought maybe I'd go to the hairdressers' and see what they can do with this."

"Jacky, *nobody'll* be able to do *anything* with that. If you ask me, you should dye it a few different colours. You know, a bit of pink, some mauve, maybe a black streak . . ."

"Thanks a lot."

"No problem. Want to get the plates out of the oven?"

"Sure. I thought I'd go home and change first," she added as she took out the plates. There were three sausages and two pancakes on each one.

"Want me to go with you?"

"I don't want to be a pain . . ."

"Hey, what are mothers for?" Kate grinned as she put another pair of pancakes on each plate and took them over to the table. "Look, it's no problem," she said as she pushed one of them across to Jacky. "I might be teasing you about all this, but I wouldn't want you to go over there by yourself."

"Thanks."

They were busy eating for the next little while, but once the initial edge of her hunger had worn off, Jacky looked across the table.

"Last night," she said. "I was wearing that jacket that Finn stitched with his magics. You weren't supposed to be able to see me when I was wearing it, but you did."

"That's right," Kate said.

"Do you think it doesn't work?"

"We should probably check it out," Kate replied.

So after breakfast, Jacky donned her blue quilted jacket and buttoned it up. She stood in the middle of the living room with Kate watching her.

"Well?" she asked.

"I can see you."

"Shit." Jacky started to unbutton the jacket.

"Wait a sec," Kate said.

Jacky paused. "What is it?"

"When I don't look directly at you, you get all fuzzy—you know what I mean?" She stood facing away from Jacky and looked at her from the corner of her eye. "And now I can't see you at all."

"Maybe it doesn't work properly in the daytime or under a bright light," Jacky said.

"Maybe. But maybe it's just that I know you too well."

"What's that supposed to mean?"

"Well, to get all metaphysical about it, we're pretty close—right? Maybe it's just that I know your vibes so well that you can't be invisible around me. I *feel* you near and since I *know* you're there, it cancels out the magic."

"What if it just doesn't work?" Jacky wanted to know.

"There's an easy way to find out," Kate said. She took her own coat from the closet and tossed Jacky the redcap. "Let's go to your place."

Jacky fingered the tear in her jeans, then straightened up and studied herself in Kate's hall mirror. God, she looked a mess. No wonder Bhruic had called her a tatterdemalion last night. She tugged the redcap on and tried to capture the various unruly locks that poked out from under it, then gave it up as a lost cause.

"Ready?" Kate asked.

Jacky nodded and followed her friend out the front door.

There was no way for them to check out people's reactions until they reached Bank Street, and then the reality of the hob's stitcheries were brought home with a very physical jar. No sooner were they standing on the corner of Sunnyside and Bank—after passing a certain oak tree with a hob fast asleep in its branches—than a woman ran over Jacky's toe with the wheels of her stroller.

"Oww!" Jacky cried.

The woman stumbled, almost overturning the stroller in her haste to back away.

"Jeez, that hurt," Jacky said to Kate.

The woman looked from Kate to where Jacky's voice was coming from, her eyes widening. Then her baby started to howl. As she bent over it, Kate quickly took Jacky's arm and hurried off across the street.

"Well, it works," she said.

Jacky looked back across the street to where the woman was still standing. The woman gazed across the street at Kate, then at the place Jacky's voice had come from until, shaking her head, she went on her way.

"This could be kind of fun," Jacky said. "Just think of the tricks you could play."

"That," Kate replied, "sounds suspiciously like what I've heard brownies and hobs are like, *not* my friend Jacky. You'd better watch yourself."

"Why?"

The answer was on the tip of Kate's tongue, but then she shook her head. She was worried that something in the hob's magic might soak through Jacky's coat and shoes and cap, that the stitcheries would change her friend, because that was the danger with Faerie, wasn't it? Mortals who entered it never came out unchanged. But she didn't have the heart to spoil Jacky's good mood just now.

Her friend stood in front of her, with her eyes all sparkling and her cheeks flushed, looking more alive than Kate could remember her being for a long time. Kate smiled. She was almost used to the unruly stubble that was all that was left of Jacky's hair now. It certainly gave her more of a mischievous air.

And who was to say that a little of the Puckish prankster in her wouldn't do Jacky a world of good? With all the weirdness going down—and with what they were going to be getting into when they headed out to Calabogie—maybe Jacky deserved to get something out of all this. Kate would just have to keep an eye on her, that was all.

"You know," she said finally. "I could get to like your new look."

"That's what I've got to watch out for?" Jacky asked. "Your bad taste?"

Kate laughed "Come on," she said. "Let's get moving."

They headed south down Bank Street, Jacky being careful not to bump into anyone, but keeping Kate in stitches with the faces she pulled at the passersby.

Jacky's apartment was the top half of a red brick duplex on Ossington Avenue, four blocks south of Sunnyside and a block and a half west of Bank Street. Her downstairs neighbour was repotting plants on the porch as they approached and looked up when they arrived. His gaze went to Kate, since he couldn't see Jacky. This pleased Jacky enormously until he began to speak.

"Hello, Kate. I think Jacky's sleeping off last night's binge."

"Binge?"

Joe Reaves brushed some dirt from his hands and nodded. "You should have heard the party she was having up there last night. Didn't bother me too much—I'm off today anyway and I still owe her for the one I threw this summer—but I'm surprised Beekman next door didn't phone in a complaint." He paused suddenly. "Say, how come you weren't there? At the party, I mean."

"I . . . uh . . . couldn't make it," Kate said slowly.

Standing beside her, Jacky felt all the fun drain out of her invisibility trick. Her stomach was suddenly tied in knots.

"Well, it sounded like some bash," Joe said. "I didn't think she had it in her, you know? She always seems so serious—or quiet anyway."

"Yeah, well . . . I'd better see how she's feeling," Kate said and moved for the door.

She opened it, then stepped aside to let Jacky go in, covering up by pretending to listen to whatever it was that Joe was saying now. She could see his lips moving, but the words weren't registering. Dragging up a smile, she nodded to him, then followed Jacky inside and closed the door behind them.

"I was out," Jacky said in a tense voice. She unbuttoned her jacket and took it off, folding it across her arm. "All night, Kate. I wasn't here."

Kate nodded. She looked up the stairs, a feeling of dread catpawing along her spine. It was a beautiful autumn day outside, but that wasn't reflected in here. A dark, indefinable sensation crept down the stairs to meet them. Something awful was waiting for them up there, she just *knew* it. She wanted to run, but forced herself to take the first step, a second, a third. When she reached the landing, Jacky pushed by her, key in hand. Here, directly outside the door, the feeling of wrongness was stronger than ever.

"Maybe we should ask Joe to come in with us," Kate said.

"And tell him what?" Jacky asked.

Kate nodded. He'd wonder were Jacky had come from and if it hadn't been her in the apartment last night, then who had it been? It would just get too complicated to explain. As Jacky fit the key into the lock, Kate wished that they had a weapon of some kind, but all the had was her little trusty Swiss pen knife that she usually carried in her jeans. The key turned with a loud snick. They exchanged worried glances, then Jacky pushed the door open.

"Oh, God," Kate murmured, moving into the apartment beside a stunned Jacky.

The living room looked as though someone had let loose a small tornado in it. Sofa and chairs were turned over, upholstery cut open, the stuffing swelling out through the jagged slits. The coffee table was in two pieces. The curtains had been torn down and left lying in a corner. Jacky's books were all pulled from the bookcase and scattered throughout the room, most of them in two or three pieces.

They could see the kitchen from where they stood. The refrigerator door hung ajar. Milk and eggs were smeared across the counters and floor. Clouds of flour and spices and rolled oats had settled over everything. Frozen meat was unthawing in bloody puddles. Shattered plates and cups and saucers covered the floor. A sour, spoiled smell rolled through the apartment.

"The Host," Jacky said, tears swelling in her eyes as she took in the ruin. "That's who did this. The Unseelie Court."

"But what were they looking for?" Kate asked.

Jacky turned to her. "Me," she said in a small voice. "And . . . and when they didn't find me, they . . . they did this . . ."

The premonition of danger hadn't left Kate yet. "Let's get out of here," she said and gave Jacky's arm a tug.

Jacky shook off her hand and moved towards the bedroom.

She was all empty inside—not the empty she'd felt when Will walked out, the empty that she had nothing important in her life, but an emptiness more akin to the aftermath of rape. Her most private place—her home—had been ravaged. Violated.

She tried to summon up an anger, but everything just seemed too bleak. As if nothing mattered anymore. All that was necessary now was to discover the full scope of the damage. Had the plush toys that had been her friends since childhood been destroyed? Had they broken the clock that had been the last Christmas present her grandmother gave her before she died? Was there anything left in one piece?

"Jacky!" Kate called softly, starting across the room.

Jacky opened the door to the bedroom. She had one moment to take in what she saw. The frame of her bed was broken into countless pieces and heaped against one wall. The dresser lay on its side, the drawers in a broken pile beside it. In the middle of the room, a huge nest had been made out of her shredded mattress, her blankets and sheets and her clothes. And rising from it, disturbed from their sleep and blinking slitted yellow eyes, were nightmares.

Their heads were wider than they were tall and their skin was brown, creased like wrinkled leather. Straw-pale hair hung in greasy strands. They weren't much taller than Jacky herself, but they were broad and squat, their heads disappearing into their torsos without the benefit of necks. Animal furs were tied about their waists, hanging to their knobby knees. Wide noses flared as they caught Jacky's scent . . . Kate's . . .

"Go her now, got her!" the foremost cried happily. His wide mouth split into a grin, revealing rows of pointed yellow teeth. "Got her, hot damn! Won't the Boss be grinning now?"

Bogans, Jacky thought.

She tried to evade the creature's grasp, but moved too late. A meaty fist closed on her arm, grip tightening until a moan escaped her lips. Her jacket fell from suddenly numbed fingers. The others were approaching. There were three of them altogether, but Jacky knew that one alone would be more than a match for her. But while they had her, they wouldn't get Kate.

"Run!" she cried. "Run, Kate!" With her free hand she snatched the redcap from her head and tossed it to her friend.

Kate caught the cap, but she didn't run. She saw the same ruin that the bedroom had become as Jacky did, but instead of a bogan gripping her friend, all she saw was a smelly old wino, gap-toothed and unshaven, with bloodshot eyes, baggy trousers, and a white shirt so dirty it was a yellow-brown. She didn't even think of what she was doing as she shoved the cap into her belt and picked up the nearest thing that came to hand. It was the brass base of a small table lamp. Three quick steps and she was in the door, her makeshift weapon coming down on the shoulder of the wino that held Jacky.

The bogan howled and Jacky pulled free of his grip. She dropped to the floor, grabbed her jacket and scuttled between the other two bogans, struggling to get an arm into the jacket sleeve. With the redcap gone, the bogans didn't look so clear anymore. She *knew* what they were, so she could still see their bogan shapes, but superimposed over them were the winos that Kate was seeing. Somehow they seemed more frightening because of that.

She got one arm in, wriggled the jacket around to get the other. She saw Kate whack the first bogan again, the base of the table lamp knocking the creature to the floor. The remaining pair had turned and were coming towards Jacky, but now she had her other arm in the jacket, pulled it on, and—

The two bogan/winos stopped in midstride as she disappeared. Jacky crept over to what was left of her bed and hefted a club-length piece of one of its legs. While the bogans stood there, trying to spot her with their day-dimmed eyes, she ran up and hit the closest one as hard as she could on its knee.

The creature cried out and stumbled to the floor as its leg gave way under him. The other bogan glanced at his companion. Before it could move, Jacky and Kate both hit it at the same time. It fell across the one that Jacky had brought down who was still clutching his knee. Jacky hit him with her club and then all three creatures lay still.

Breathing heavily, the two friends looked at each other. The moment of action had cut something loose inside them. The shock of the ransacked apartment and the attack faded before the self-sufficient feeling that rose in them. Going to the Giants' Keep and rescuing the Laird's daughter . . . it didn't seem quite so impossible now.

"Are they . . . are they dead?" Jacky asked, breaking the silence.

Kate shook her head as she still tried to catch her breath. "I don't know. Jacky, what the hell are a bunch of winos doing in your apartment?"

"Winos?" But then Jacky realized that Kate was seeing them without the benefit of hob stitcheries. "Stick the cap on your head and see what they really are," she said.

Kate worked the cap free from her belt and put it on. The lamp base fell from her hand.

"Oh, jeez," she mumbled. "What *are* they?"

"Bogans," a voice said from the living room before Jacky could answer. "And that was well-done indeed, though you're lucky it's day and not night, for you wouldn't have had such an easy time of it if they'd been completely awake."

Jacky and Kate turned, adrenaline pumping in a rush through their systems once more. Kate took a step back, but Jacky touched her arm.

"It's okay, Kate," she said. "This is Finn."

"At your service," the bearded hob replied with a small bow, "though you don't much seem to need it at the moment."

"What are you doing here?" Jacky asked.

"Following you. I chased after you all night, but couldn't find the right thread to lead me to you. Then the sun came up and I fell asleep. When I woke, my stitcheries told me that you'd passed right below me while I was snoozing. So I followed the new thread and it led me here—too late for the rescue that you didn't need, which is just as well, for I don't know if I would have been so quick to attack three bogans—even in the daylight." He regarded each of them admiringly. "Oh, yes. It's good to know there's still a hero or two left in the world."

"This is my friend Kate Hazel," Jacky said before she remembered that she should have thought up a speaking name for Kate, rather than giving away her true one. Jacky didn't exactly distrust the little man, but with that touch of feral slyness in his eyes, she wasn't sure if she trusted him completely either.

"Kate Hazel," Finn said. "Hazel—that's the Crackernut, you know. A wise tree—not so lucky as the Rowan, to be sure, but sometimes clever thinking will take you farther than ever luck could. It's more dependable, too. I'm pleased to meet you, Kate Crackernuts.''

Kate looked at him, not really hearing what he was saying. She turned to Jacky.

"We have to get out of here, Jacky," she said.

Her gaze flickered to the bogans. The one she'd struck was definitely dead. Thick greenish-red blood was pooling around its head.

"I think I'm going to be sick," she added.

Finn nodded. "We'd best go quickly. Where there's a few bogans, likely there's more. No sense pressing our luck, even if we do have a Jack with us."

Jacky swallowed hard. She too couldn't look at the bogans for long without feeling queasy. But she felt no regret at what they'd done.

"Let's go," she said.

Taking Kate's arm, she led the way out of the apartment. On the stairs going down, she took the redcap from Kate's head, thrust it into the pocket of her jacket, then removed the jacket once more and carried it in her free arm.

"I believed you," Kate was saying as she let Jacky lead her down the stairs. "I *really* did. I mean, there was the cap and that biker last night who was there and then wasn't, depending on how you looked at him. But I thought it was . . . I don't know. Not real at the same time. Do you know what I mean?"

She paused at the bottom of the stairs and looked back up at the door to Jacky's apartment. Finn had closed it behind them.

"I guess I'm not making much sense, am I?" she said.

"Lots of sense," Jacky assured her.

"Not to me," Finn said, but Jacky glared at him so he shrugged and said no more.

Jacky opened the front door and stepped out onto the porch, tugging Kate along with her. Finn followed right on their heels. Joe Reaves looked up from his pots and plants, his eyes widening. Jacky had forgotten the way she looked, but she wasn't going back upstairs for new clothes now.

"What happened to you, Jacky?" Joe asked. "That *is* you, isn't it?"

"Oh, it's me all right."

"Going punk on us, are you? No wonder your party was so rowdy last night." He grinned, but his humour faltered when Jacky just looked at him. "Look, it's your hair. . . ." he began.

"It's okay," Jacky said. "I'm just going through a bit of a weird time and I'm kind of in a hurry, Joe."

"Hey. No problem. See ya around."

Jacky nodded and led her two companions off down the street, leaving her downstairs neighbour on the porch, scratching his head. It was weird, she thought. She knew she should be scared, and she was, but not like she should be. It was more a cautious kind of being scared that would keep her from getting too cocky. But those things back in the apartment . . .

"Are you going to be okay?" she asked Kate.

"Yeah. I think so. But, jeez. Talk about wimping out."

"You didn't wimp out, Kate. You saved the day." Jacky found a grin for her friend. "Just like the valiant tailor."

Kate came up with a small smile. "I'm sorry about your place, Jacky."

"Me too. I think maybe we shouldn't wait the couple of days Bhruic told me to. We should take off now."

"What did the Gruagagh tell you?" Finn wanted to know.

"Oh, this and that. What will those bogans do when they find us gone and one of them dead, Finn?"

"They won't be so gentle with you next time," the hob replied. "None of the Host will."

"Great." Jacky glanced at Kate. "Are you up for Calabogie?"

Kate nodded, not quite trusting her voice. Jacky squeezed her arm.

"I know what you're feeling," she said.

"I'm still going," Kate told her.

"I know you are. And I love you for it."

Walking a couple of paces behind the pair, Finn shook his head. They were either brave or fools. What they had just undergone in Jacky's apartment could not begin to prepare them for what was waiting in the Giants' Keep. And yet, brave or foolish, they were going all the same. And he—knowing himself to be a fool—was going with them.

The Laird of Kinrowan's folk owed them that much and since he was the only one of the Laird's folk present, since he'd put the burr in Jacky's cap and set her on the road, it seemed only right and proper that he be the one to see it through and go with them. But oh, he wasn't happy about it. Not one bit.

CHAPTER
9

"You okay?" Kate asked.

Jacky nodded. Or at least as okay as could be expected, she thought, now that the immediate need to be brave and sure of herself had passed. When Kate had been falling apart back at the apartment, it had been easy to take on the leader's role. But now Kate was more herself and Jacky was wondering where she'd find the courage to go on. When she thought about those things in her apartment . . . the bogans . . .

"You and me," she said to Kate. "We're like a couple of yo-yo's—first you're being strong for me, then I'm doing it for you, and now we're back to square one again. I just hope that we don't ever fall apart at the same time."

"There's always your friend Finn."

"I suppose."

The two of them were sitting in a window booth at Hitsman's, a restaurant on Bank Street that was just a couple of blocks south of Jacky's apartment on Ossington. They were trying to come up with a plan of action. Finn was at the pastry counter, deciding what he wanted to have with his tea. He looked like a small, but ordinary man, rather than the hob Jacky knew, but that was a part of the—what he called—glamour that he wore in the everyday world.

They had chosen the restaurant, rather than Kate's apartment, because it was more public and therefore—they hoped—

safer. The Unseelie Court preferred to act in lonely places and at night, Finn had assured them.

"It's past noon now," Kate said. "Do you think we can get to Calabogie and do whatever we have to do before it gets dark?"

Jacky shook her head. "I've got a pretty good idea where the Keep is from Bhruic's map, but I don't know how long we'll be inside looking for the Horn. Actually, I don't even know *how* we'll get inside, or what we'll find there." She looked out the window and watched a couple of cars go by. "Actually," she added as she turned back to Kate, "it seems like a pretty crazy thing to be doing in the first place. I mean, it's not like we're really the heroes that Finn keeps talking us up to be."

"Maybe we should get a gang," Kate said. "We could call it 'the Gang' and . . . ." She was looking out the window and broke off as Finn joined them, his plate loaded down with a half-dozen pastries.

"You're going to get sick eating all of those," Jacky said.

"Finn," Kate said before he could reply to Jacky. "There's a guy standing there beside the Fresh Fruit Company—on the left, see him? He's been there for about ten minutes now, not doing anything except just hanging around."

"Where?" Jacky said, sticking her face close to the window to have a look.

The man met her gaze from across the street, a half-smile on his lips, then stepped back around the corner of the building and out of sight. Jacky was left with a vague memory of a tallish man in jeans and a jean jacket, clean shaven with tousled chestnut hair.

"Now you've done it," Kate said. "You've let him know we're on to him."

"It's not so bad," Finn said. "That was Arkan Garty—one of Crowdie Wort's foresters."

"Does that make him one of the good guys or one of the bad guys?" Jacky asked.

"Crowdie Wort owes his allegiance to the Laird."

"Then why was his forester watching us?"

"I . . . ." Finn looked from Jacky to Kate, then shrugged. "I don't know. The air is thick with rumours. Foremost is the fact that you mean to rescue the Laird's daughter, so the

Laird's folk can only wish you well. But at the same time they know that you've been to see the Gruagagh, so those more devious-minded amongst the Seelie Court are suspicious that your rescue attempt is just a story and that your presence in the scheme of things spells yet another disaster for the Laird's folk.''

"You're kidding, right?''

Finn regarded Kate seriously and shook his head. "With winter coming, the loss of the Laird's daughter is the worst thing that could have happened to us. Without her to sing the lockspells on Samhaine Eve, we could all lose our lives that night.''

"You're not making sense,'' Jacky said. "What're lock-spells? What happens on Samhaine Eve?''

"The dead walk. Not just the sluagh, but all the dead, and we have no power against them. They are jealous of our living, so on that one night we hide in places locked safe with spells that only the Laird's daughter knows.''

"Well, she must have learned them from *someone*.''

"She did. From her mother. But the Lady Fenella is gone and Lorana has no daughter yet to pass the knowledge on to. Without the lockspells, we are easy prey for the dead. They wouldn't kill us all, but enough so that we could not survive the winter being harried by the Unseelie Court.

"We were stronger once. We had revels on Samhaine— gathery-ups and all manner of fun. The Lady Fenella led us in the songs then and just the singing of them kept the dead at bay. But now . . . now we hide in safe places locked tight with spells and wait for the night to pass without a smile or a laugh passing our lips. For those that the dead catch on Samhaine Eve—they become the sluagh of the Unseelie Court. There is no afterlife for them, and no borning again.''

"Bhruic said Lorana was the green soul of Kinrowan and he was its heart,'' Jacky said. "Wouldn't he know the songs, too?''

"No one knows what the Gruagagh knows or doesn't,'' Finn replied, "except for maybe the Laird himself. But Dee-gan is none too happy with the Gruagagh for losing his daughter, and there's few in the Seelie Court that would trust the wizard enough to let him lead us in the songs.''

"I *like* Bhruic,'' Jacky said.

"He can glamour anyone to like him."

"It wasn't magic—it was just, oh, I don't know. I just *know* he's not evil." She hoped.

"And I know that you're not evil," Finn said, "but there's still some that won't trust you simply because you've been the Gruagagh's guest."

"I'd like to meet this Gruagagh," Kate said before an actual argument broke out between Jacky and the hob. "Why don't we go see him now on the way to my place?"

"We can't," Jacky said. "He said I shouldn't return."

"Well, could you at least show me his Tower?"

"It's just a house," Finn said, shaking his head. "And Learg Green's too dangerous for us now."

But Jacky, feeling obstinate, disagreed. "Oh, we can look at it," she said. "We can go to Kate's place by following the river. It won't be dangerous just to walk by," she added to Finn. "There'll be lots of people in the park—jogging, playing ball, walking their dogs and babies."

"And how many of them will belong to Gyre the Elder?"

"Who knows?" Jacky replied with a shrug. "But you said yourself that they wouldn't do anything when there's lots of people around." She eyed his plate of pastries. "So eat up and let's get going."

Finn looked down at his plate. "I'm not hungry anymore."

"Maybe this wasn't such a good idea," Kate said while they were getting a bag for Finn's pastries. The hob was still sitting at their table, staring morosely out the window.

"It'll be okay," Jacky said. "I think he just likes to build things up."

"He didn't build up those guys back at your apartment."

Jacky frowned. "No. But we've got to wait until tomorrow morning to leave anyway and it doesn't matter which way we go back to your place—there's the chance that the Host'll be watching us no matter how we go. It's tonight at your house that's worrying me—not getting there. Thanks," she added as the red-haired girl behind the counter gave her the bag with Finn's pastries in it.

"We could have a party," Kate said.

"What?"

"A party. Tonight. We'll invite all the bruisers we know and have all sorts of protection."

Jacky laughed. "We don't know any bruisers."

"Then we'll just have to meet some."

"I think you're almost serious."

Kate winked. "Maybe I am," she said as they returned to their table to collect Finn.

By day, the park across from the Gruagagh's Tower was a different place. There were no bikers, no giants. The Rideau River moved slowly along the south side of the green. Dried reeds rustled in the breeze. The swans were gone now, but flocks of ducks floated close to shore, hoping for handouts. There was a football game in progress as they entered the park's Bank Street entrance. The teams were short—only five men to each side—but what they lacked in numbers, they more than made up for in enthusiasm. On the path by the river two women with strollers were walking. A jogger moved around them onto the grass as he passed and soon left them behind.

"That's the Gruagagh's Tower," Jacky said, pointing it out. "The one with the back yard all overgrown."

"It looks deserted."

"I think it is—except for him." A big shout came from the football players as one team scored a touchdown. "And there are your bruisers," Jacky added with a grin.

"I think I'll pass," Kate said. "Can we walk closer to the house?"

"Sure. Only don't expect to see much from here because . . ." Jacky paused as Finn plucked at her shirt sleeve. She shifted her jacket from one arm to the other as she turned to him.

"We can't stay," he said urgently.

"Why? What's wrong?"

"I don't know. I just feel it in my bones. There's a glamour lying thick and deep here, just waiting to snare us."

"A glamour . . . ?"

Jacky looked around as she spoke. The day, the park and the people in it, all seemed so ordinary. But then she remembered what had been waiting for them in her apartment, and last night's mad flight from the biker flooded her mind. God, she could be so stupid. What was she doing, bringing them

all here when she knew—she *knew*—how real the dangers
were? It was as though ever since the attack in her apartment,
she'd decided that they'd won the war. But all it had been was
one small engagement.

"Which way should we go?" she asked.

"Back the way we came," Finn replied. "Come. Quickly
now."

Jacky nodded. But it all felt so normal still. Her pulse
drummed, but there was nothing that she could see that she
could even pretend was a danger to them.

The women with their strollers were almost out of sight.
The football players had just begun a new play. The quarter-
back pumped his arm and the ball went spinning, a high,
long pass in their direction. The ball was caught about twenty
yards away from where they were standing, the man who
caught it grinning with pleasure. His teammates worked to
block the tacklers that were coming in from either side. And
then—

Then it was too late.

Before Jacky could turn, before she could put proper use
to the swiftness stitcheries that Finn had sewn into her sneakers, they were upon her. At the last moment, their forms
shimmered. They were college-aged men and bogans at the
same time. The foremost man threw the football aside and
hit her hard, scooping her up under his arm. Her breath went
out of her in a whoosh at the impact. Her jacket, with the
redcap in its pocket, went flying from her grip.

"Got her, got her, GOT HERRRRR!" her captor roared.

There was no more attempt at disguise as the bogans
charged through the park, their captive held fast. They cheered
and shook their fists in the air. Kate saw Finn go down as he
tried to rescue Jacky, and then a bogan fist smashed into the
side of her head and sent her spinning.

She tried to rise, the whole world turning dizzily around
in her vision, but another of the creatures stopped long enough
to kick her in the stomach. She buckled over, bile rising in
her throat. When she finally pulled herself up to her knees,
the park was eerily empty except for herself, Finn who lay a
half dozen paces away from her, and the blue jacket that
Jacky had dropped. ·

Kate crawled towards Finn. Every movement of her head

brought tears of pain to her eyes. Her stomach felt as though something had ruptured inside. When she finally reached Finn, it took all her strength to turn him over. A trickle of blood escaped the corner of his mouth and he was so pale that she was sure he was dead. His face had almost a greyish cast to it and he lay so still . . .

She brought her cheek down to his face and held it there until she was sure that what she felt on her skin was his breath. So he was alive at least. But Jacky . . . She looked despairingly in the direction that the bogans had taken her friend.

What in God's name could she do now? She looked back at Finn, but he was in worse shape than she was. There was no one she could think of that she could go to with a story this weird. The police would think she was nuts. God, *anybody* would think she was nuts.

Slowly she got to her feet and stood swaying. She'd get the jacket. And then she'd—God, it was hard to think—then she'd what? Her gaze fell on the unkempt lawn of the Gruagagh's Tower. Then she'd make *him* help her. She started for the jacket when a voice stopped her.

"Fools."

She turned slowly to find Crowdie Wort's forester regarding her.

"Moon and stars!" he cried. "What possessed you to return here? Surely you'd at least guess that they were waiting for you?"

Kate decided to ignore him. Step by careful step she made her way to the jacket, picked it up. She saw the redcap sticking out of the pocket and plucked it out, putting it on as she turned back. Arkan Garty's glamour fled him as the redcap settled in place.

He was no longer tall and no longer . . . human. His skin was a reddish brown, his head narrow and more a fox's than a man's. The jeans and jean jacket he'd been wearing had now become some weird tunic and trousers that looked as though they were just leaves and feathers and bits of fur all stitched together.

"Did they tear out your tongue, girl?"

Kate took a quick breath to settle the drum of her pulse. It didn't do much good. There was a weird light in the forester's eyes that seemed to say that he was capable of anything, but surprisingly, she wasn't afraid of him.

"What . . . what do you want?" she asked.

"I was charged to watch out for you."

"Well, you didn't . . . do such a good job, did you?"

The lights flickered dangerously in his eyes. "If you'd kept to safe ways—" he began, but Kate cut him off.

"Did you see where they took her? Where they took Jacky?"

He shook his head. "I lost them on the Laird's Road—but they left a trail that I can follow. It's not easy to miss the stink of a bogan and a pack that big will be easy to track. I came back to see if you needed help."

"And . . . now?" Kate asked, wishing her head didn't ache so. "Are you going after them?"

"That's for Crowdie Wort to say when I bring news of this afternoon's work to him."

Kate nodded, then wished she hadn't moved her head. She looked at the forester and thought of what Jacky had told her—how none of them would help the Laird's daughter. Instead they left it up to someone like Jacky who wasn't even close to their match in magics and strength. Anger boiled up in her.

"Well, go bring him your news," she said softly. "And then crawl back into whatever hole it was that you came from. You and your people seem very good at arriving after the fact. And then you talk the talk, real good. But me—when I look at you—all I see is a snivelling coward."

As she spoke the last words, she slipped on Jacky's blue jacket. From the look on Arkan's face, she knew that its stitcheries were working for her as well.

"Little hob spells won't help you against the Unseelie Court!" he cried. "Don't you think that we'd *want* to help our own Laird's daughter? But the Giants' Keep won't be breached by strength alone and the Wild Hunt will track down and kill anyone who tries. The luck's gone out of us—just as it's run out for your friend. Moon and stars, if there was something we could do, we would. But the Host outnumbers us five to one and they have the Hunt!"

"Screw you too!" Kate called to him as she started painfully across the park towards the Gruagagh's Tower.

"Come back! Crowdie Wort will want to talk to you."

Kate glanced back to see him testing the air with his nose, looking for all the world like a dog casting for scent. Scent! She pushed herself to move more quickly. The jacket might hide her from his sight, but it wouldn't do anything about her scent. And she didn't dare let him take her back to this Crowdie Wort—whoever *he* was—because the Host had Jacky now and if she didn't do something about rescuing Jacky, no one would. Arkan and his people would let her rot in the Giants' Keep the same way they did their own Laird's daughter. Clutching her stomach, she broke into a halting trot, aiming for the Gruagagh's Tower.

When she reached the hedge at the back of the Gruagagh's yard, she paused to look back again. Arkan had guessed her destination and was coming for her at a swift lope. She turned quickly and made her way across the overgrown back yard, reaching the Gruagagh's door at the same time as Arkan did.

He grabbed at the air around him, but Kate pressed close to the door and hammered on it, then dropped to her knees so that Arkan's arms cut the air above her head. Open, she told the door, but it was too late. Arkan's hand brushed her shoulder, returned and grabbed her, hauling her to her feet.

"You *will* come with me," he told her. "Moon and stars, girl! It's for your own good. The Gruagagh's not to be trusted."

Kate brought her knee up into his crotch and he doubled over, losing his grip on her. She hadn't been sure what kind of equipment a being like Arkan had between his legs and was happy to see that he had the same weakness as an ordinary man. She backed up against the door, flinching at the wild look in his eyes. His gaze raked back and forth across the small back porch, vainly looking for her.

"Damn you," he said from between clenched teeth. "I'm not the enemy."

Before Kate could reply, the door opened behind her and she tumbled backwards. Strong hands caught her and set her back on her feet. She looked up, and up, and there was Jacky's Gruagagh looking down at her from his height. Apparently the jacket's properties didn't work against him. He gave her a long considering look, then turned his attention to Crowdie Wort's forester.

"And who is the enemy?" he asked softly. "The untrustworthy Gruagagh, perhaps?"

The change in Arkan was immediate. Kate could see the fear fill him.

"Oh . . . oh, no . . . your reverence . . ."

For a long moment the Gruagagh simply stared at Arkan, then he said: "Bring the hob here to my door—and gently."

Arkan nodded quickly and backed away. When he reached the bottom step of the porch, he turned and bolted for the park. Kate was sure he was going to just keep on running until he'd put as much distance as he could between himself and the Gruagagh, but he surprised her. When he reached Finn's still form, he lifted the hob up into his arms and hurried back.

"They mean well," the Gruagagh said to Kate as they watched Arkan return with his burden. "But these are hard times."

"I . . . I suppose. It's just . . . I don't know. I'm not really sure who's who and on what side just yet. Jacky's told me everything she knows, but that doesn't seem like a whole lot."

"Jacky," the Gruagagh breathed.

Arkan reached the porch just then and the Gruagagh took the hob from him, cradling Finn in his arms.

"Go back to Crowdie Wort and spill your tale," he told the forester. "And mark you don't forget to say a word or two against me while you're telling it."

"Oh, I wouldn't, your reverence."

"Not much you wouldn't," the Gruagagh said.

He turned and motioned for Kate to close the door and she did, getting a small sense of satisfaction out of seeing the fearful look that was still on Arkan's face as she shut the door in his face. But then she remembered why she was here, and where here was, and who here belonged to. Jacky said she'd liked the Gruagagh, but he seemed downright scary to Kate. Who was to say he *could* be trusted?

"Will . . . will Jacky be all right?" she asked.

Laying Finn down on the windowseat, the Gruagagh lifted the hob's eyelids, one by one, to examine the rolled-back eyes. Only then did he glance at Kate. He seemed to consider her question for a long moment, but rather than answering it, he turned back to the hob again, making no reply.

CHAPTER
10

Kate found the Gruagagh's Tower to be just as strange as Jacky had described it. Wherever she looked she got the sensation of things sliding out of sight just as she settled her gaze in their direction. Ghostly furnishings that were here and then gone. And in the darker corners, there was movement of a different sort. She thought of rats and spiders and moved closer to the windowseat where the Gruagagh sat beside Finn. But when she looked at the Gruagagh's grim features, she found little comfort there.

He had pulled a fat leather shoulder pack from under the windowseat and was now removing various vials, poultices and blankets. The pack, Kate thought, didn't look big enough to hold half of what he was taking out of it. The first thing he did, once he pushed the bag back under the windowseat, was mix up some concoction in a small bowl which he then handed to her.

"Drink this."

"No way," she said, beginning to back away.

"It won't harm you," he said.

Kate hesitated for a moment longer, then gingerly took the bowl from him. The liquid smelled awful, a sweet cloying smell.

"You came to me for help, did you not?" he said when she simply held the bowl, not drinking. His voice was mild, but his gaze was fierce.

76

"Okay, okay," Kate said.

Screwing up her face, she drank it down. Whatever it was tasted as foul as she'd imagined it would, but no sooner had she swallowed it, than a warm feeling spread from her stomach, easing her queasiness and clearing her head.

"What is this stuff?" she asked.

Rather than replying, the Gruagagh indicated that she should help him with Finn. While Kate held the hob's head and the bowl, the Gruagagh forced small amounts of the liquid between Finn's lips, stroking the hob's throat to make him swallow. Once some colour had returned to the little man's wan features, Kate stood to one side as the Gruagagh tended Finn's hurts. He rubbed a lotion into the bruises on the hob's torso and applied a poultice to the little man's brow. Then he turned to Kate.

"Your turn," he said. "Sit here and lift your shirt."

Kate felt uneasy again, pulling up her shirt in front of the Gruagagh, but he maintained a professional, detached attitude throughout the examination, gave her an ointment to rub onto the bruise, and pronounced her as fit as she could be after a run-in with a pack of bogans. He made a bed for Finn in the corner of the room, using the blankets he'd pulled from his seemingly bottomless pack, then brought out two mugs and a thermos which began to steam from its mouth as soon as he opened it and placed it on the windowsill between himself and Kate.

Kate looked at his grim face, then at the thermos. The blend of tea smelled delicious. She wanted to ask him where she could get a bag like his, but another look at his face froze the question in her throat. She turned instead to look out the window at Windsor Park—what Finn had called Learg Green.

"I take it you don't get many visitors," she said after a few moments.

"Few enough." He poured some tea, already mixed with milk in the thermos, and handed her a mug.

"Thanks."

It was far better tasting than the earlier concoction, but spread a similar warmth from her stomach as she took a sip. She looked around the kitchen. The sense of hidden movement and ghostly furnishings wasn't so pronounced anymore.

"What do you *do* in here?" she had to ask.

"Duty didn't always confine me to my Tower," he said. "Time was I was as free to roam as any of the Seelie Court. But times are hard and with the Laird's daughter gone, Deegan won't let me risk Kinrowan's Heart in rescue of her—for all that she's his daughter and her loss pains him deeply."

"What is this Heart?"

The Gruagagh smiled. "Why, it's myself. I'm the Laird's heart—the Heart of Kinrowan."

"I don't understand."

"You've been told how our glamours and magics have diminished, haven't you?"

Kate nodded, though from all she'd seen this past day, she had to wonder what those magics were like before they had diminished. They seemed to work pretty good so far as she could see.

"Well, diminished or not," the Gruagagh said, "what we have left is maintained by my focus. This Tower of mine is built on a criss-cross of leys—straight tracks. Do you know the term?"

Kate nodded. "They're supposed to be lines that connect sacred sites, aren't they? So the Tower's like Stonehenge?"

"Exactly—but on a much, much smaller scale than that holy place. They ley lines are conduits of power—earth strength, moon strength, water, fire and air. I take those strengths and spread them through the Laird's land. They are all that keeps us from fading."

"Jacky said it has something to do with people not believing in you anymore."

"That is an old argument that has never quite been resolved," the Gruagagh replied. "Many faerie, and some few mortals, have put forth the thought that we are sustained by your belief. All I know is that in this time of disbelief—disbelief that the Seelie Court exists, at any rate—we are diminished from what we were. I have also heard it put forth that the cause lies in the fact that we live in a borrowed land."

"In your homeland," Kate asked, "do the people still believe?"

"More so than here," the Gruagagh replied, "but I see your point. Our numbers are fewer there as well. The issue becomes more clouded, I think, by our unwillingness to accept that we depend upon mortals for our existence.''

Well, she could see that, Kate thought.

''So you're Kinrowan's Heart,'' she said to change the subject, ''and the Laird's daughter is its soul. Were you lovers?''

Something flickered in the Gruagagh's eyes, but Kate couldn't quite read what it was. Pain, perhaps. Or anger? But it was gone as quick as it had come.

''We have played the part,'' he said, ''when the seasons demanded it. But mostly we are friends. If Lorana had a husband, then I would be freed of my duties. But until that day . . .''

Kate wondered what he mean by ''when the seasons demanded it.'' It sounded too much like animals going into heat, but then she realized that he must mean holy times, like solstices, May Eve and Samhaine.

She stole a glance at him as he stared silently out the window, his face set in stern lines again. She remembered Jacky telling her about his scar, and how it didn't matter when he relaxed. But when he was tense like he was now, it made him seem so grim. It was probably time for her to go. But first . . .

''Are you going to help me find Jacky?'' she asked.

The Gruagagh turned to her, his gaze looking into unseen distances. Then his eyes focused and he regarded her steadily.

''For that we must go upstairs,'' he said.

Kate glanced at the hob where he lay sleeping in his nest of blankets. ''What about Finn?''

''Let him rest. Hurt as he is, he won't be much help in what you must do anyway. Now come. We've spent too long gossiping. The day's almost done.''

Kate set her tea mug down and looked out the window. It was getting late. Fear pinprickled through her as she realized that she'd have to set off at night to find Jacky. The Gruagagh was at the door, his pack hanging from his shoulder by its strap. Turning from the window, Kate hurried to join him and followed him upstairs.

They went up one flight of stairs, then another. Around them the house was quiet. Kate still thought she saw sly movements in the darker shadows, but the small shapes made no sound. Their own footsteps echoed strangely in the empty halls and rooms as the Gruagagh led her into a third-floor bedroom. Except for the lack of furnishings, the house didn't look deserted. There was no dust. The plaster walls were clean. The wooden floors and trim were highly polished.

"How come no one lives here?" she asked. "Besides you, I mean."

"It's too close to Faerie. I have shared it with others from your world, but they always find the place too . . . unsettling, and quickly move."

"Why don't you just buy it—I mean in the real world?"

The Gruagagh turned to her. "Which is more real?" he asked. "Your world, or Faerie?"

"I . . ."

"But I do own this house—in your world as well as in my own."

"Well, why don't you furnish it, then?"

"You see only what you are meant to see. Come here now."

He motioned to the window and opened it as she came to stand by him. For a long moment she clung dizzily to the windowsill. She had expected to see the street below and the tops of the trees that lined it, their leaves all red and gold and stiff with autumn. Instead the entire city was spread out below her in miniature. From Britannia in the far west end all the way out to Vanier; from Parliament Hill on the Ottawa River to the north, all the way south to where Bank Street became Highway 31.

What she saw didn't seem possible. Vertigo counteracted the effects of the potion that the Gruagagh had given her earlier and her stomach roiled. The Gruagagh touched her arm, steadying her.

"Is . . . is this real?" she asked in a small voice.

"The city—or our view of it?" he replied with a touch of amusement.

"You know what I mean," she said.

The Gruagagh nodded. "Both the city and our view of it is real. We see it from a gruagagh's Tower, you see. A gruagagh must be able to view all of his Laird's land at once in times of need—a time such as this."

"There's my house," Kate said, pointing it out.

"Be still a moment," the Gruagagh said.

He leaned far over the windowsill. As the minutes ticked by, Kate shifted her weight from one foot to the other, but the Gruagagh never moved. Then, just as she was going to say something, he made a sound.

"Ah."

"Is that a good 'ah,' or a bad one?" she asked.

"That depends," the Gruagagh said as he pulled back from the windowsill. "Do you see that big building there in Cockle Tom's Garve?"

"In what?"

"Cockle Tom holds the area you call the Glebe in trust for the Laird, in the same way that Crowdie Wort holds this area in which we are now."

"Oh. What building? That's the Civic Centre at Lansdowne," she said when he pointed it out again. "Is that where they took Jacky?"

The Gruagagh nodded. "Until tonight. Then I think they will move her to their Keep."

"In Calabogie—where Lorana is?"

"We know the Hunt's Horn is there," the Gruagagh replied, "but not where the Laird's daughter is. That was why Jacky was going to steal the Horn."

"Yes. But couldn't you just 'find' Lorana like you did Jacky?"

The Gruagagh shook his head. "They have the Laird's daughter too well cloaked with glamours for me to find her."

They were silent for a long moment. Finally Kate sighed and stirred.

"Well, I suppose I should get on with it," she said. "Do you have any ideas?" she added as the Gruagagh led the way back downstairs.

"Strength will do nothing, but slyness might. What you must do is steal in and find her, secret and sly, then make your escape as best you can."

Kate paused on the stairs. "Oh? Is that all? What a perfect plan. Now I wonder why I didn't think of it."

The Gruagagh looked back at her. "What do you want of me? Should I wave my hands and set all to right?"

"That'd help."

"My magics don't work that way."

"So how do they work?"

The Gruagagh sighed. "In secret ways—mostly. The time for greatspells has passed this world. Remnants remain—such as the Wild Hunt's Horn and the moon dancing of long-stones—but little enough that ordinary faerie may use."

"But you're supposed to be this mighty Gruagagh. Everybody's scared to death of you."

"What magics I have," he said, "cannot be used for such things. If I forsook my responsibilities, there are things I could try, but I dare not. Shall all of Kinrowan's faerie fail so that I might rescue your friend?"

"You're no better than the rest of them," Kate said. "You're just looking for saps like me and Jacky to do your dirty work for you."

"Not so."

There was a dangerous flicker in his eyes that Kate ignored. "Not so?" she began in a squeaky, mocking voice, but then she thought better of it.

There was more that she wanted to say. It lay on the tip of her tongue, but she bit it back. What was the point? She had Jacky to think of right now. And there was the Laird's daughter—she deserved better, too. So for them, but especially for Jacky, she'd go and do what she could. But not for Faerie, and certainly not for the Gruagagh.

She pushed by him. "See ya later, chum. I've got things to do."

She went down the hall until she found the room where Finn was still sleeping. There she collected the blue jacket and the redcap that had started it all.

"Kate," the Gruagagh said as she headed into the kitchen. "Jacky chose to go—no one made her."

"That's because no one else would go."

The Gruagagh shook his head. "Because no one else *can*."

"Okay," Kate said. "I understand you've got to stay here and, you know, be that focus and everything, but what about the other faerie? Why don't *they* do something?"

"Because of the Hunt. Contrary to your nursery tales, we do have souls. But those that are taken by the Hunt lose them."

"So it's okay for me or Jacky to lose ours?"

"Fear doesn't seem to paralyze you as it has my people, nor are you trapped by your duties as I am."

"You didn't answer me."

"No one forces you to do anything," the Gruagagh said.

"It's kind of late for that, isn't it? They've *got* Jacky now."

"It was not something I planned."

Kate thought about how Finn had warned them to stay away from the Gruagagh's Tower and nodded slowly.

"When you say the Hunt takes your soul," she said. "Does that mean you become one of the restless dead like on Samhaine Eve?"

"No. The Hunt feeds on the souls they catch."

Kate shuddered. "But still . . ."

"We've lost our heroes, Kate. All we have left are hobs and brownies, little folk that can't even stand up to bogans, never mind the Hunt of Gyre the Elder and his kin. They have had to hide and steal about for so long now that they don't know *how* to be brave. It will take new heroes to show them and our heroes have always been mortal."

"If you're expecting *me* to be their role model, you're in for a rude surprise. I'm not a hero."

"No? But still you're going out to rescue your friend. I'd call that brave."

"Yes, well . . ." Kate flashed him a quick awkward smile. "I've got to go."

"Be careful, Kate Crackernuts."

Kate regarded him for a long moment, then nodded. Slipping on the redcap, she ducked out the back door. She stood in the back yard and looked up at the darkening sky. It would be full night before she even got back to her place to get her car. She was about to put on the jacket and head out, when a familiar figure stepped out of the hedge. Arkan Garty, Crowdie Wort's forester.

"Don't *you* start again," Kate told him before he could get a word out.

Arkan held his hands open in front of him. "I want to go with you," he said. "I want to help."

"Is that what your boss told you to say?"

Arkan shook his head. "I haven't left the Gruagagh's yard since you went in. I've been thinking about all you've said and I . . . I'm ashamed. . . ."

His voice trailed off and he looked so uncomfortable that Kate took pity on him. She wasn't really sure why she did what she did, because she only half-trusted him, but perhaps it had something to do with what the Gruagagh had said to *her* about heroes. She didn't feel particularly heroic, but it took some doing to admit you were wrong—she knew that from the times she'd had to do it herself. If Arkan Garty was willing to help, then she should be willing to give him the chance.

"Come on, then," she said. "Time's running out."

Arkan fell in step beside her and they hurried on down the park, making for her apartment.

"What do they call you?" he asked as they reached the spot where Belmont met the Rideau River.

That was a polite way of putting it, Kate thought, remembering what Jacky had told her about faerie and their speaking names.

"Kate," she said. "Kate Crackernuts," she added with a smile. She had to be nuts. "Welcome to my nightmare."

"What?"

The rock and roll reference was lost on him, Kate realized, but she didn't try to explain it. How did you explain Alice Cooper to someone from Faerie?

"Nothing," she said. "It's just something that Jacky and I say to each other when the going gets weird, and tonight, Arkan, let me tell you, the going's definitely gotten weird."

The foxish head nodded beside her. The gloom of twilight gave Kate the eerie feeling that she was hurrying through the dusk with a werefox. Definitely a weird night. And it was just starting. Hang in there, Jacky, she thought. The cavalry's on the way. All two of us.

CHAPTER
11

Jacky was hanging in there—just.

When the bogans snatched her, she'd literally gone numb with panic. She saw first Finn, then Kate go down, and then the bogans' rush took them out of the park into a mad dizzying run through Ottawa South's streets.

Don't they *see*? she remembered thinking as the bogans swarmed by a man walking his dog, children playing in a schoolyard, two workmen taking a coffee break. But there was Faerie and her own world, she realized, and only with a redcap could you see into the former from the latter. A redcap or . . . She'd dropped both cap and jacket when the bogans grabbed her, but she still *saw*.

Touched, she thought. Touched by Faerie and I'll maybe always *see* now. I've gone fey.

The bogan gripped her so tightly, and the heavy reek of his body odour was so strong, their speed so dizzying while she bounced against the creature's rock-hard skin . . . it all combined into a frightening whorl that spun inside her until Jacky did something she'd never done before. She fainted dead away. When she finally came out of her faint, sick and feverish with its aftereffects, there was cold concrete under her and a pool of bogan faces spinning slowly around her, slowing down like a merry-go-round running out of steam until she could make out each hellish face with a clarity she wished wasn't hers.

She almost passed out again, but knew she couldn't afford to. She had to get OutOfHere RightAway. As the dizzying feeling came over her again, she bit down on her lower lip and forced her eyes to stay open. Her stomach churned, but she remained conscious.

The creatures that surrounded her weren't all bogans, or at least they weren't all like the things that she and Kate had fought back in her apartment. Some were twins to those ugly squat creatures, but there were others . . . Something like a naked woman, emaciated and grey-skinned, her ribs protruding and the skin drawn tight across her features, snuffled close to Jacky's head. Pale eyes regarded her with a hungry gaze. When the creature leaned close and licked at Jacky's cheek, she choked on a scream and whipped her head aside. The bogans laughed at that.

"Don't like you much, Maghert, hot damn!"

The grey woman-like thing hissed. "Give usss a tassste."

A bogan gripped Jacky's head and held it while Maghert rasped her tongue across Jacky's cheek. Jacky moaned and that made the bogans laugh some more. Thick fingers poked at her stomach, squeezed her thighs, jabbed at her breasts.

"Plump enough to spit her, sure," one of the bogans said. "Don't need to stew this one, no, hot damn!"

Twig-thin creatures capered and danced just beyond the circle of bogans. The grey-skinned hag's tongue felt like it was licking the side of her face raw. There was a trollish, slopebacked creature, its body festooned with shells that clattered as it bent close, a gap-toothed leer splitting its face. Jacky tried to curl herself into a ball, but the bogans just pulled her straight, poking and prodding. Saliva spilled from their mouths when they laughed. Their reek made the air unbreathable.

"I like mine raw," a rumbling voice announced to a new chorus of rough laughter.

A bogan pulled Maghert away from her, cuffing the hag across the head. "Leave a bit for the rest, you old whore," he muttered.

One of the tiny twig-thin creatures sidled close and began to pluck at her hand. "Just a finger," it moaned before it too was cuffed aside.

"Leave her be!" the large bogan who'd pulled the hag

away roared, taking command. "Leave her alone, or I'll spike the lot of you, just watch if I don't, hot damn!"

A chorus of protests arose.

"Greedy!"

"Spike you, arsebreath, hot damn!"

"We'll stew *you*, Skraker!"

"She's for the Big Man," Skraker growled. He stood over Jacky, like a cougar straddling its prey, and slowly faced down the crowd of angry creatures. "She's for the Boss and maybe he'll share her and maybe he won't."

"We're hungry now!" a bogan protested.

"Give her to usss," Maghert whispered, creeping closer again.

Skraker leapt forward and began batting the creatures indiscriminately with his big fists until they all backed off. He spared Jacky a glance. When he saw she was still breathing, he paced back and forth across the concrete floor, glaring at his companions until they broke off into small groups of twos and threes and fell to arguing amongst themselves. Then he sat down near Jacky to keep guard.

The smell of her made his stomach rumble, but he knew better than to go against the wishes of the Big Men. Human prey was rare. Take too many, and the men were out hunting you, pretty damn fast. So the few humans that fell into the clutches of the Unseelie Court went first to the Big Men. But there were always scraps. And it was those that followed orders that got the scraps, hot damn.

For a long time after the creatures had stopped pawing at her, Jacky lay still, hardly daring to breathe. The sheer horror of her predicament had unnerved her to the point where it was all she could do to keep herself from fainting dead away again. The touch of the hag's tongue, all those hands and fingers, squeezing and prodding, and the talk of spits and stews . . . She shuddered.

She'd thought the worst thing that could happen would be to fall into the clutches of the Wild Hunt. Now she knew better. Anything to do with the Unseelie Court was a horror. She felt weak and sick, hardly able to lift her head. But slowly, as she was left alone, the terror was pushed back. She realized that she had to plan, she had to *do* something to get

away. There would be no rescues. And now, with this first-
hand experience, she understood the reluctance small hobs
like Finn had about confronting the Host.

Think, she told herself. Remember all those fairy tales you
read as a kid. If these things are real, then whatever the good
guys used to destroy them probably worked too. Except they
all had magic swords, or talking cats, or handsome princes
to rescue them. All she had was herself. A very scared self.
Against twenty or more monsters. She started to shiver again,
then pinched herself hard. The pain was enough to help her
focus on trying to think of something, instead of just curling
up and dying.

She sat up, very slowly, stiffening when the big bogan
nearby turned quickly around, nostrils flaring. Jacky thought
her heart would stop as he stared hungrily at her. She lifted
a hand to her face and wiped away the drying, sticky saliva
that was there. Her stomach did a flip as she frantically wiped
it off her hands. The bogan grinned.

"Try and run," he said, "and I'll take off one of your
legs, the Big Man be damned!"

"I . . . I . . ." Jacky began, but she couldn't get anything
out except for that one syllable, and it sounded like the kind
of squeak a mouse made.

"Bet you taste good," the bogan muttered as he turned
away from her. "Hot damn!"

Her sitting up had brought a circle of the other creatures
around them that quickly dispersed when the bogan guarding
her snarled at them.

She had to wait, Jacky told herself. Wait for the right moment. They'd left her with her sneakers and the hob magics
stitched into them. If she could just get a little bit of a head
start, they'd never be able to catch her . . . would they? But
the waiting was hard. Time dragged, the way it always did
when she was waiting for something. And then there was the
bogan sitting so close to her, its body odour traversing the
distance between them in sickly waves. And the other creatures that were snuffling about—the hag and the little feral
twig creatures, the trollish thing with the clattering shells,
and the other bogans. Not to mention the knowledge that one
of the Big Men was on his way . . .

To try to keep her mind away from all of that, she studied

her surroundings. This was the Civic Centre, she realized. An indoor rink that was also used for concerts. She'd gone to a zillion rock shows here. Was this the Ottawa home of the Host? Were they into rock and roll? When she looked at the creatures around her, she didn't think they'd be out of place in a heavy metal band's video.

An image popped into her mind of the bogans tying her to a spit while an announcer's voice spoke overtop, "And now, new from the Unseelie Court, here's 'Eating Out With Jacky' . . ." And there was the hag, singing lead, with bogans on guitars and that big thing with the shells on drums, looking like some psychotic's version of a Muppet . . .

She shuddered and knew that she couldn't wait for the right moment. She had to make it for herself. If she stayed here much longer, she was just going to wither away. It was bad enough that she kept feeling faint. If she kept that up, the next time she woke up it might well be in a stew.

She got ready to get up and run for it and damn the torpedoes. It was time for GoJackyGoJackyGoJackyGo. But then there came a commotion at the far end of the arena and all her resolve drained away in a rush. This was it. The Big Man was here for his dinner. Except it wasn't the giant. It was more bogans and they were dragging in a new captive.

Oh, God—they've got Kate, she thought, then knew a moment's relief when she saw that the short brown curls on the Host's new victim belonged to a man. At least she thought it was a man. She squinted, trying to get a better look, realizing at the same time that she was passing up her best chance of GettingOutOfHere. The new captive seemed to be wearing some kind of feathered boa. Then wonder snared her completely and she couldn't move.

It was a man all right, only he didn't have a man's arms. In place of them he had two big black wings. They didn't give him the majesty of any angel, as she might have thought if someone had described a winged man to her. Instead the wings hung awkwardly from his shoulders, the feathers drooping. A kind of rough brown tunic covered his torso.

As his captors dragged him closer and the creatures already present began to howl, one of those old fairy tales she'd been trying to remember came back to her. It was the one about the seven brothers who were turned into swans. At the end of the story, after their sister had woven nettle shirts for each of them, they all turned back into men. All except the youngest. He was left with a swan's wing because his sister hadn't had time to finish one sleeve of his shirt.

This swan man was like that, she thought. Except his sister hadn't finished off either one of his sleeves. Then she had no more time to think, for the noise of the creatures became deafening as they howled and those howls rebounded from the lofty ceilings.

"Royal blood!"

"HotdamnhotdamnHOTDAMN!"

"Oh, give usss, give USSSSS!"

The bogan guarding Jacky lunged to his feet. He caught hold of one of Jacky's arms and hauled her up, dragging her with him as he went to meet the newcomers. With his free fist he batted away at the shuffling creatures that were trying to get at the swan man.

"Back off, shitheads!" he roared. "BACK OFF!"

When he reached the newcomers, he threw Jacky at the swan man and turned to beat off the snarling, howling crowd of creatures. Jacky fell to her knees, feeling the painful jar of the concrete floor all the way up to her jaw at the impact. Her face struck the swan man's arm—wing?—and she choked on the feathers. A bogan hand grabbed the short spikes of her hair and pulled her head roughly back.

"Hey, Skraker!" the new bogan leader said. "This thing of yours is trying to eat our boy."

Jacky's captor turned with an evil grin. "I'll eat you, arse-breath, if you don't give me a hand with these shitheads."

Jacky and the new captive were unceremoniously hauled off to one side where the bogan remained on guard, while the rest waded into the excited creatures that were trying to get through Skraker. There was more of the Host here now, Jacky realized. A lot more. Their numbers seemed to have tripled. The fact of her doom pressed down on her like a heavy weight once more and she leaned back against the wall, fighting back tears. The noise in the arena made it impossible to think. The squabbling creatures, each more horrible than the next, just brought home her helplessness.

It was a good ten minutes before some semblance of order returned. Skraker came back to stand guard over Jacky, talking with the leader of the new patrol of bogans. They both kept an eye on the ever-growing crowd of the Unseelie Court.

"The Big Man better get here soon," Skraker said, "or I'm throwing both of them out to that crew—minus a leg or two."

"Hot damn!" the other bogan said. His own patrol was now lost in the crowd out on the floor. "A taste of Royal blood—now wouldn't that be something."

Skraker shook his head. "The Big Men don't eat those. Keep 'em for trade. But I'd eat 'em, sure would. You know, Gooter, sometimes I just . . ."

The two bogans drifted mercifully out of Jacky's earshot. She closed her eyes, but that brought no relief. Something touched her shoulder, light as a feather . . . She blinked her eyes open wide to see that it *was* a feather, or at least the tip of a wing. She almost laughed at the weirdness of it all. But she knew that if she laughed, that'd be it. GameOver and That'sAllFolks. Because she'd never stop.

"You're a mortal," the swan man said.

Jacky pinched herself again, waiting for the pain to bring her down to earth. At this rate, between the Host and herself, she wouldn't have an unbruised spot on her body. She managed to nod and then cleared her throat.

"You . . . you're not?"

He shook his head. "I'm Eilian Dunlogan." The look on his face said, Don't you know me? Then a half-smile, self-mocking and bitter, touched his lips, adding, And why should you? "I'm the Laird of Dunlogan's son," he said aloud.

Jacky nodded wisely, still in the dark, though there was something familiar about the name. "I'm Jacky Rowan," she said. "What did they do to your arms?"

"Do? They did nothing. All the Lairdsblood can wear the shape of a swan or seal. They've just used one of their damned spells to bind me between shapes. They're not stupid, though you wouldn't think it to look at some."

"But can't you just . . . just fly away?"

Eilian shook his head. "These wings could never support a man's body. You see, with my wings, I can't get the nettle tunic off, and with the tunic on, I can't complete my change. It's a very clever trap—especially for such as these."

Jacky bit at her lip. This seemed a little too simple.

Couldn't she just pull the tunic off? She started to move forward to do just that, when Skraker strode up behind her and cuffed her across the back of the head. She sprawled across Eilian, knocking the breath out of him.

"Don't you be getting no ideas, little smellsogood, or I swear I'll leave you less one arm, hot damn!"

Two black wings encircled her, trying to give what comfort they could. It was little enough, but it was something.

"And you too, you Royal shithead," Skraker warned. "I've got eyes in the back of my head and in the sides and up my arse. You can't chew snot without me seeing you—got that? The Boss'll be here soon and you can take up any complaints with him. He might spike your new little friend there, but you'll be safe enough. Until we get to the Keep. And then, oh hot damn, you better start worrying about then, for what's Dunlogan got that's worth trading you for? Royal soup's the better bargain, I'm thinking."

He strode back to Gooter, chuckling. Slowly Jacky sat up. She turned in her winged embrace to look at Eilian, trying hard not to cry or let her fear show. Surprisingly, it was getting easier. She wondered if she was just getting used to her predicament—they said people could adjust to anything—or if it was because she wasn't alone anymore. She wouldn't wish this on anyone, but she couldn't help feeling better for having company. And even if Eilian did have wings, he was still worth looking at. He was handsome in a rugged sort of way—which was odd, because his bones seemed very delicate. It was the warmth of his eyes, she decided, that helped most. That, and the laugh lines around his mouth.

"It . . . it was really bad being here by myself," she said.

Eilian nodded understandingly. "I'm glad to have met with you, Jacky Rowan, even in circumstances such as these." The wing tightened around her shoulders.

Jacky blushed. God, I'm such a mess, she thought. But then Eilian was just as disheveled as she was.

"How did they catch you?" she asked.

Eilian sighed. "They put up a sign that said, 'Fools wanted,' so naturally I ran over to see if they could use me." He grinned at her smile, then sighed again. "No, it wasn't as bad as that—though not by much. How much do you know of Faerie?"

"Not a whole lot."

"But you know of the two Courts? How the Seelie Court grows weaker, year by year, while these creatures grow ever more bold and strong?"

Jacky nodded. "Bhruic told me about that."

"Bhruic? Bhruic Dearg, the Gruagagh?" Eilian regarded her sharply, then shook his head. "Laird love a duck, I *am* a fool. Why, you're the reason I came south from my father's Court."

"Me? But you don't know anything about me."

"The whole of Faerie's a-buzz with word of you, Jacky. And by your name, I should have guessed who you were. You're the hope of Kinrowan, aren't you? The one who means to storm the Giants' Keep?"

Hysterical laughter started to bubble up in Jacky and it was only with a great effort that she kept it down. "Look at me," she said. "Do I look like I could storm anything?"

His warm eyes regarded her for a long moment, and then he said, "I think so, yes."

Jacky could feel another blush coming on, so she looked away and cleared her throat. "Does . . . ah, the Host have a weakness?"

"For flesh, mostly."

"No. I mean, something that can hurt them."

"Cold iron's best—sword or axe or knife—though it wouldn't do one much good with this lot. Faerie that dwell in the city have become acclimatized to the sting of iron over the years—though they give up something in exchange for that immunity. Their lifespans are shortened and they're no longer as hardy."

"Isn't there anything else?"

"Well, there's the wood, berries and leaves of the rowan— like your name—and the red thread stitcheries of a skillyman hob. Salt, too. Running water slows them—they can't cross it easily. And if they're chasing you, turn your coat inside out and you'll lose them for a time."

"Oh." It was starting to come back to her. "What about using the name of God?"

"That, I'm afraid," Eilian said, "is a story passed around by your church and not based on truth." Jacky looked disappointed even though she wasn't an avid churchgoer. "Faerie," he went on, "are more like mortals now than we'd like."

As they talked, Jacky had been keeping an eye on the various creatures of the Unseelie Court, particularly on the two bogans, Skraker and Gooter.

"I've got magic sneakers," she whispered when she was sure neither of them was paying any attention.

"What?"

"My shoes—a hob made them magic."

"Ah." Eilian said with a nod. "Swiftness stitcheries."

"If I can get a bit of a headstart, I'll bet I could outrun them."

And then, she thought, I'll just take off my shirt in the middle of Bank Street and turn it inside out so that the Host can't find me. No problem.

"And you want me to create a diversion for you?"

Jacky shook her head. She was still watching the two bogan leaders. They were beginning to get into an argument.

"How tight's that nettle shirt?" she asked.

Understanding gleamed in Eilian's eyes. "Too tight for wings to loose, but not so bad for you."

Jacky bit at her lip, gauging the distance between the bogans and themselves. The argument between the bogan leaders was intensifying. She chose a moment when Skraker roared something at Gooter and then gave the other bogan a shove that sent him sprawling.

"Let's do it," she said.

Quickly she turned and grabbed hold of his shirt. The nettles stung and pricked her fingers, but she ignored that. She jumped to her feet and hauled the shirt free. Black feathers sprayed around her as though she and Eilian had just had a pillow fight.

"Go!" she cried.

Before her eyes, the son of Dunlogan's Laird became a black swan. The big wings, no longer useless, beat at the air, lifting him from the ground. Howls broke out all around the hall, but neither Eilian nor Jacky stayed to look. He rose high into the air, out of their range, while Jacky pulled herself over the balustrade that separated the rink from the spectators' tiered seats and took off at a run.

Feets don't fail me now, she thought.

The swan flying above her made encouraging noises. Her sneakers slapped the concrete floor. She was really moving, she thought. And thank Finn for that. Behind her and following on the main floor of the arena was the horde of the Unseelie Court's creatures, their growls and snarls raised in a cacophony. But she was GettingOutOfHere and adrenaline was pumping through her. She had magic shoes and no one was going to catch her.

She was almost to the closest doorway and well ahead of their pursuers. She started to pluck at the buttons of her shirt, feeling stupid, but willing to give anything a try if it would help. Eilian cried down at her. She didn't look up, just kept running.

GoJackyGoJackyGoJackyGo!

The door was near, and she was through it. There were stairs coming up. Don't trip, she warned herself. Behind her the Host was gaining on her. She tried to slow down as she neared the top of the stairs, didn't think she'd make it, then saw why Eilian had been calling to her. One of the Big Men was coming up the stairwell.

He wasn't as big as Gyre the Younger, but he still stood fourteen feet tall, with legs and arms like small tree trunks and a big barrel of a torso. The hair on his head was a grizzle of grey brown, his beard hung half-way down his chest. He looked up, grinning a big gap-toothed grin.

The thing with the shells back in the arena must be his little brother, Jacky thought, looking at that grin. She didn't have time to think anything else. Didn't have to plan. Didn't even know she'd do what she did until she was already doing it.

As she reached the top of the stairs, she launched herself right at the giant. He tried to bat her out of the air, but she was moving too fast. She hit him hard, toppled him, then rode him down the stairs, holding onto his beard for purchase. They hit the bottom of the stairs with a jarring crash. There was a sound like something splintering, but it was a wet splintering sound, then Jacky lost her grip and went rolling, skidding to an abrupt stop against a wall.

For a long moment she lay there, half-stunned. She looked back, seeing the Unseelie Court swarming at the top of the stairs. Right at the bottom, the giant lay with his head cracked open, blood and greyish brain matter splattered all around his head.

All she could do was stare, her stomach doing flip-flops. Then Eilian dove down at her, startling her with a sharp call and a brush of a black feathered wing. Right, she thought. She was GettingOutOfHere. She was GoJackyGoing.

She got to her feet and started to run again, hardly realizing that the only thing that had saved her during her moment of disorientation back there was that the Unseelie Court had been just as shocked as she was by the death of one of the Big Men.

A giant, Jacky thought as she ran. Holy shit! I killed a giant!

There were doors up ahead. She reached them, coming to a stop by running into them. Holding them open for Eilian to fly through, she slipped out after him and was stunned by the fact that it was night outside. Night! God, she'd been in there with the bogans for hours.

She undid the last button of her shirt and was tugging it off so that she could turn it inside out—and wouldn't that just add to her fashionableness—when something landed on her back. She screamed, arms trapped by her shirt. Hot breath touched her neck. Tiny twig-like fingers plucked at her hair and skin. Then Eilian dove from the sky and knocked the little creature off with a blow of his wings. Jacky took a few stumbling steps away and saw that the one twig-creature wasn't alone. There was a great deal of rustling movement in the shadows behind its fallen form.

Hardly daring to breathe, she finished taking off her shirt, backing up all the time. Eilian kept dive-bombing the creatures, keeping them from her as she turned the shirt inside out, put it back on, started to button it. She was mostly down the steps outside the Civic Centre now.

"Eilian!" she cried.

Things scurried by her, but they didn't see her. Jeez, it works, she thought. But then she realized that it probably worked on Eilian as well. She tried to spot him, but the sky was too dark.

"This is getting stupid," she muttered as she started to undo the buttons again. But she wasn't going to go on without him. If she had a lucky name, then he was her lucky piece, because without him she might never have gotten out of there. *Nor* killed the giant.

"Eilian!" she cried again, pulling the shirt free.

Suddenly there was scurrying all around her. Eilian dropped from the sky and took his own shape by her side. The bogans and other creatures from inside the Civic Centre were at the top of the steps and still coming out of the glass doors. In the darkness around Jacky and Eilian, the twig-creatures were gathering their courage, hissing and chattering amongst themselves.

"What do we do now?" Jacky asked her companion.

He turned to her, but then they both heard the squeal of tires and saw a car turn in from Bank Street. Its headlights caught them, blinding them both. Jacky heard the driver downshift a gear and the car leapt forward with a roar of its engine.

"Oh, shit," Jacky said. "They're going to run us down."

CHAPTER
12

It was dark by the time Kate and Arkan Garty reached Kate's apartment. The street was quiet. Up the block a couple of teenagers were just turning the corner, their voices loud in the still air. Kate and Arkan waited until the pair were out of sight, then approached the house, keeping to the shadows.

The darkness didn't trouble Kate half as much as the fact that the windows of her apartment were all lit up. For one moment she thought, maybe Jacky's there. But then she realized that if Jacky *was* there, it was in the company of the Unseelie Court.

"What's the matter?" Arkan asked.

Kate glanced at her foxish companion. "There's someone in my place."

Arkan's eyes narrowed as he studied the lit windows. He moved into the deeper shadows alongside her neighbour's house, pulling Kate with him. Softly they crept across the driveway, hugging the walls of Kate's building as they stole up to a window to have a look. One glance was all that was needed.

"Bogans," Kate said, seeing them for what they were with Jacky's redcap on. "Shit. Now what're we going to do?"

"We don't need to go inside, do we?" Arkan asked. "It's only your car we came for."

"But the keys are inside. I've only got my housekeys on me."

"Where is the car?"

"We *need* the keys to the car," she told him. "Or do you know how to hotwire it?"

Arkan nodded.

Kate stared at him. "You *do*?"

"Just because I'm part of Faerie, doesn't make me stupid."

"Yes, but you don't drive cars."

"Who told you that?"

"Well, no one. It's just in all the stories."

A foxish grin stole across Arkan's face. "There weren't many cars in Shakespeare's plays either."

"Yes. But they didn't have cars back then . . ."

Kate's voice trailed off. Right, she thought. And they didn't have them when people were putting together fairy tales either. Andrew Lang hadn't been much of a hotrodder and Perrault wasn't known for his skill in the Grand Prix. And when she thought of Jacky's Wild Hunt . . . black-leathered bikers on their Harleys . . . Well, who was to say what a denizen of Faerie might or might not know?

"Well, let's get to it," she said.

She led the way to where Judith, her VW, was sitting in the driveway. She cast a quick glance back at the apartment—that was her life the bogans were prying into now, *her* personal space—then she bit down the rising tide of resentment. Jacky was what was important now. Not her apartment.

They reached the Volkswagen. The driver's door opened with a small protesting creak. The interior light didn't come on, but that wasn't through any forethought on Kate's part. It had simply burnt out a few months ago and she hadn't bothered to replace it yet.

"Judith," Kate hissed. "Help us out and I'll get you an oil change as soon as this is all over—I promise."

Arkan regarded her with amusement, then slid in. He bent down to fiddle with the wiring under the dashboard, leaving Kate to stand nervously by the open door. She plucked at the quilting of Jacky's blue jacket that she was still carrying. Something caught her gaze, a rapid movement in the corner of her eye that was there and gone so quickly that she barely registered it. She started to put on the jacket.

"Arkan," she warned. "There's something out here."

When she had the jacket on—and it had better be working, she thought—she moved away from the car, looking for something she could use as a weapon. No pack of bogans was going to bonk her on the head again and leave her sprawling, thank you very much. The next-door neighbour's rake was leaning against his back porch.

All right, Kate thought as she made for it, going on tiptoes. There. She saw something move again. Just around the corner of her house. And she could hear whispering now. A dry, unfamiliar smell was in the air. Her fingers closed on the rake. The weight of it was comforting as she soft-stepped her way back to the car. She was about to call out to Arkan—just to ask what was taking the great faerie car booster so long— when she saw something big and bulking glide from the front of the house and move soundlessly towards Judith's open door.

Not feeling brave, just angry, the rake tight in sweaty hands, Kate moved in behind the creature. She let him get nice and close to the car, then swung the rake behind her head and brought it around in a sweeping arc until it connected with the head of whatever it was that had been sneaking up on Arkan. The wet sound as it hit and the jarring blow that went right up her arms to her elbows killed any satisfaction she got from her deed.

The big shape dropped like a felled ox. The rake dropped from Kate's hands. She saw Arkan jump at the double sound, knocking his head against the dashboard.

"It's . . . it's okay," Kate called in a loud whisper. "I got him."

Whatever "him" was. She bent to retrieve the rake just in time to see a collection of small lanky creatures come scurrying from around the back of the house. Oh, shit, she thought. There had to be fifteen or twenty of the things. They were small, shadowy shapes, like the silhouetted branches of winter trees come to life. As they scurried forward, that dry smell was in the air again . . .

"Look out!" she called to Arkan as she ran to meet them, trusty rake in her hand.

The VW's engine coughed into life on the heels of her words. Kate threw the rake at the foremost creatures and watched them go down. The ones immediately behind fell over their leaders as she bolted for the car. Arkan had it in

gear and was backing down the drive while she was still opening the door.

"Wait for me!" she cried.

She hauled the door open and flung herself inside. Arkan
floored the gas pedal and Judith lunged out onto the road,
passenger's side door flapping. Pulling in her feet, Kate
grabbed the loose door, kicked away a couple of over-zealous
twig-creatures, and banged it shut. She braced herself as the
VW skidded to a stop. Arkan slammed the car into first and
Judith leapt forward, leaving rubber on the pavement behind
her. The sudden movement thrust Kate against her seat. Arkan changed smoothly from first to second, into third. Looking out through the rear window, Kate saw that they were
losing the little band of creatures.

"Nice timing," she said as she turned around to face front
once more. "God, what were those things?"

"A kind of goblin."

Arkan shot her a foxish grin. The longer she was with him,
the more he looked like good old Reynard, Kate thought.

"A kind of goblin," she said. "Lovely." Another thought
came to her. "Can you see me?"

Arkan shook his head, concentrating on his driving. "No.
But I can hear your melodious voice, so I assume you're with
me."

Oh, he was a cool one, Kate thought. But she liked him
better like this than as the penitent that had met her at the
bottom of the Gruagagh's garden.

"So what kind of goblins were they?" she asked as she
worked at removing the blue jacket in the confines of the car.

"Gullywudes. Tree goblins."

Kate stifled a giggle. She'd almost heard gollywogs. Then,
jeez, she thought. Look at me. I just fought off a pack of
these gullywudes, knocked a bogan for a loop, and I'm sitting
here laughing about it all. Like it happens every day. Another
giggle slipped out and she put a firm clamp on any more.
This wasn't funny. This was being hysterical.

As she finally got the jacket off, Arkan gave her a quick
glance.

"I know, I know," Kate said. "I shouldn't be, but I'm
feeling giddy as a goose."

"It often happens when mortals mix with faerie," Arkan

replied. "It's a natural reaction—no different from how you'd feel after a moment of stress. And you've just been going through both."

"So now you're a doctor?"

"It's a common fact—did no one tell you?"

"No."

Great, Kate thought. First I've got to worry about Jacky turning into a trickster, and now I'm turning into a giggly basketcase. And then she had something else to worry about.

They had just reached a red light at the corner of Sunnyside and Bank and Arkan took a sharp right without stopping. Kate grabbed for the handle hanging above the passenger's door. Okay. So it was legal to make a right on the red in Ontario, but couldn't he at least have stopped and *looked*? There was a sudden blare of car horns and screeching brakes behind them.

"It'd be nice if we made it there in one piece," she muttered.

Arkan didn't take his gaze from the road. "It'd also be nice if we didn't have the Hunt on our tail."

"The Hunt . . . ?"

Kate turned again and saw three Harleys coming around the corner, cutting off more cars.

"Oh, jeez." She turned back. Lansdowne Bridge was coming up fast. "I thought you had to be from Faerie or wearing a redcap to see them?"

"You do. I'm from Faerie and you're—"

"Wearing a redcap. Yeah. I know. But the other cars on the road aren't, and they can see 'em." She looked back. The three bikers were gaining.

"Take off the cap and you'll see what they see."

So she did. There were still three motorcycles back there, but now they looked like they were being driven by members of a biker gang like the Devil's Dragon.

"The last time I took off the cap they just disappeared."

"Were they in traffic?"

"No, there was just one of them, sitting on my street, watching the house."

"They occupy space," Arkan explained, "even when invisible. In traffic like this they must be seen or a car might run into them."

"So they can be hurt?"

"It would . . . delay them."

They were up the hill of Lansdowne Bridge and barrelling down the other side. Still going fast. Very fast. Kate wondered if some hob skillyman had stitched a few spells into Judith's tires.

"What do you mean 'delay them'?" she asked.

"They would have to find new bodies."

"New . . . Right. Forget I asked." She leaned back to look out the rear window again. "I thought all nine had to be together before they attacked?"

"True enough. But there only needs to be one, if all they are doing is following us."

Kate turned to face front, swallowing thickly. "Turn here," she said as the entrance to the Lansdowne Park came up.

Arkan's response was instantaneous. They went around the corner on two wheels, tires screeching again.

"Jeez!" Kate protested. "Be still my heart."

But then the headlights picked out a small figure standing in the middle of the parking lot by the Civic Centre. It was Jacky! The head with its freshly-cropped stubble was familiar now. Only why was Jacky standing there in her bra, with her shirt hanging from her hand? Arkan put the gas pedal to the floor once more.

"Arkan!" Kate cried. "That's Jacky!"

"I know. But she's not alone."

Not alone? Kate fumbled for the redcap and stuck it back on her head. The scene in front of her leapt into a new focus. There was Jacky, as before, but there was a man standing with her as well. All around them was a whole forest of gullywudes. Down the steps of the Civic Centre a flood of bogans and other creatures were descending. Not to mention that behind the VW was a third of the Hunt. Perfect. All they needed was a Big Man or two and—

She braced herself, hands against the dash, when she realized what Arkan was up to. As he neared Jacky and the man, he suddenly hauled left on the wheel. The responsible little VW lunged at the nearest bunch of twig-creatures, mowing them down. And like bundled twigs, the gullywudes just seemed to come apart, spraying bits of wood everywhere. Arkan spun the wheel some more. The tires screeched on the pavement as he swept through a second, third, fourth grouping. He made three circuits, then brought the car to a shrieking halt.

This time Kate was prepared. As soon as the car stopped, she had the door open. She scrunched herself forward against the windshield, hauling the seat with her so that Jacky and her friend could get into the back.

"Kate!" Jacky cried. "Oh, God, am I glad to—"

"In, in, IN!" Kate cried.

For the first time Jacky seemed to be aware of the three members of the Hunt. The howl of their bikes was loud, drowning out the cries of the Unseelie Court as it rushed down the final steps of the Civic Centre. Without another word, Jacky crawled into the back seat, tugging on Eilian's arm until he followed her. The Laird's son was still getting in when Arkan pulled away again.

"Now where to?" he asked nobody in particular.

"Some place safe," Kate said quickly. She was leaning over the back seat, grabbing for Jacky's hands. "You're okay! How'd you get out?"

Jacky was a-glow with excitement. "I did it, Kate! I killed a giant. I really did. Just like you said I would."

"You *what*?"

"I killed . . ." Then the wonder of it all drained from Jacky's features as what she was saying hit home. She'd killed someone. Dead. Finito binito. "Oh jeez," she said.

A sick feeling came over her. She began to tremble, her eyes filling with tears, and she buried her face in the shoulder of the young man sitting beside her. Kate looked at him, wanting to know who he was and what part he'd had in all of this, when Arkan demanded her attention again.

"Mistress Kate," he said. "*Where* safe?"

He was still going around in circles in the parking lot. The headlights kept giving them glimpses of hordes of gully-wudes, bogans, hags, shelly-coats and goblins. And the three riders of the Hunt. As he drew near to the latter, Arkan suddenly dropped into a lower gear and tromped the gas pedal, twisting the wheel at the same time. The VW's fender clipped the nearest biker's machine. He went flying, his bike skidding across the pavement in a shower of sparks.

"I don't knooooow!" Kate wailed. Everything was just too wild.

"A restaurant," the stranger in the back seat said. "A place with lots of light and many people."

"Right," Arkan said. He straightened the wheel and aimed Judith for the gates of the parking lot.

Kate took a deep steadying breath, let it out. Too quickly, but it didn't matter. It had helped.

"That won't stop them . . . will it?" she asked.

"With Cormoran dead," the stranger said, "the creatures have no leader to tell them what to do. They naturally avoid the well-lit public places of man, even in a moment such as this—unless ordered otherwise."

"She really killed one of the Big Men?" Arkan asked.

"Wart-nosed Cormoran—and she did it all on her own."

"Damn," Arkan muttered. He brought the car out onto the road in a skidding turn, then immediately slowed down and tried to blend in with the sporadic traffic on Bank Street. "That I'd like to have seen."

"What about the Hunt?" Kate asked. "Won't they still follow?"

"They'll follow," the stranger said.

Kate sighed. "And they won't be happy. We hurt one of them back there."

Jacky's companion shook his head. "Discomforted him, perhaps, but the riders of the Hunt are not so easily hurt."

"Then what'll stop them?"

"The death of Cormoran for the time being. That will leave them without orders. They'll follow us, I think—the two that are still mounted, the third if his machine was not too badly damaged—but I doubt they'll do more for now."

He was stroking Jacky's head, comforting her as he spoke. Jacky's shirt was a bunched-up ball in her hands.

"Who are you?" Kate asked.

"My name's Eilian. Your friend rescued me from the Unseelie Court."

Kate shook her head, her lips forming a soundless "wow." *Her* Jacky had done all this? She reached through to the back seat, adding her own comfort to what Eilian offered, even if it was just a pat on the knee.

"Maybe you should get her shirt on," she said. Through

the rear window she could see two of the Hunt following. "If we want to get into a restaurant, it'd help."

Understatement of the week. The way they all looked, she wondered where they'd all get into. And why wasn't Jacky wearing her shirt? She probably shouldn't even ask. There was so much going on that she felt left behind while everything spun past her in a dizzying whirl.

They were over Lansdowne Bridge again, past Sunnyside, going down the long hill that Bank Street made before it crossed the Rideau River at Billings Bridge. This was an odd strip—antique stores and bookshops side by side with bicycle and auto repair stores. Hillary's Cleaners came up on the left. The South Garden—a Chinese restaurant—was on the right, but it was too quiet.

"There!" Kate cried, but Arkan was already pulling into the parking lot.

It was a Dairy Queen. Lit up. Huge glass windows so that you could see all around. And even this late in October, it had lots of people in it. Kate leaned over the back seat as Arkan parked the car. Jacky sat up and squirmed into her shirt, looking the worse for wear with her rumpled clothes and the wild stubble of her hair. But she seemed to have a grip on herself again. A small smile touched her lips.

"Let's all go to the Dairy Queen," she sang quietly to the tune of its familiar advertisements.

"You ass," Kate said, but she could have kissed her.

She opened the door on her side and stepped out nervously. She looked around once, twice, then spotted the two black riders sitting on their Harleys in the lot of the gas station across the street. Arkan looked at her from over the roof of the car.

"Are you sure we'll be okay here?" she asked him.

Arkan shook his head. "No. But what else can we do?"

Good question, Kate thought. She stood aside as Eilian and Jacky disembarked, then led the way into the restaurant.

CHAPTER
13

Jacky and Kate brought each other up-to-date over burgers, fries, and thick milkshakes. They interrupted each other constantly with "You didn't!"'s and "I would've died"'s, much to the amusement of their faerie companions.

Hilarity sparked between them and Kate thought about what Arkan had said about how Faerie effected mortals who strayed into it. She worried, remembering snatches of old tales telling of poets driven mad by faerie queens and the like, but it was too hard to remain sensible with the way Jacky was carrying on and the giddiness that continued to bubble up inside herself.

There'd been no need to worry about how they looked. The mid-evening Dairy Queen crowd, while not quite as scruffy as the four of them, were hardly fashionable. Polyester and jeans were the order of the day. One man in green and yellow plaid trousers, mismatched with a red and blue striped windbreaker, set them all off again.

Double-dating at the DQ, Kate thought as she looked in the window and caught the reflection of the four of them in their booth. Then she saw the third rider pull up in the parking lot across the street. He put his machine on its kickstand beside the other two bikes, then walked over to where his companions stood under a billboard advertising Daniel Hechter sweatshirts.

What struck Kate first and foremost was that she wasn't

wearing the redcap at the moment. It was sitting on the table beside the wrappers of the two burgers that she'd devoured.

"How come I can see them?" she asked, interrupting Jacky in the middle of explaining why she'd been standing with her shirt in her hand when they'd picked her up. "The riders," she added at the general collection of blank looks her question gathered. "I can see all three of them and I'm not wearing the cap."

"Each time you see into Faerie it becomes easier," Arkan said. "Not for all, mind, and quicker for some than for others. You see us don't you?"

"Yes, but—"

"Think of it as a painting that you've had for years. A nice landscape, perhaps. One day someone comes in and says, 'Look at that face in the side of the hill,' and from then on you'll always be aware of that face. Because you'll *know* it's there."

"It's that simple?"

"No," Arkan replied with a grin. "It's faerie magic."

Kate aimed a kick at him under the table, but missed.

"What're we going to do about them?" Jacky asked, indicating the riders with a nod of her head. "We won't be able to do anything with them following us around."

"We must lose them," Eilian said.

Arkan shook his head. "Easy to say, but impossible to do."

"The Gruagagh would know a way," Jacky said.

"But he told you not to go back."

"That was before, Kate. He was afraid they'd get my scent or something. Well, they've got it now, so what harm would there be in going to ask him for advice?"

"One does not go lightly against the wishes of a gruagagh," Eilian said.

"We're not really going to do that," Jacky insisted. "It's just that things have changed. Nothing's the same anymore. We can't go sneaking into the Giants' Keep, because with the Hunt following us we might as well just step right up and ring the front doorbell. We need a trick to get by them and the Gruagagh's the one to give it to us."

"We do need something," Eilian agreed.

"How did you know about Jacky?" Kate asked the Laird

of Dunlogan's son, speaking as the thought came to her. "What brought you here looking for her?"

They all looked at him and even Jacky saw him as though for the first time. There was a look about him that set him a cut above the common. His hair was the black of the feathers she remembered, his eyes darker still. A Laird's son was like a prince, wasn't he? Eilian smiled as though reading her thoughts. Unfortunately, Jacky told herself, by that reckoning, the only princess around here was Lorana. Rescuing her could make this whole thing into a regular fairy tale.

"There is a story told in Dunlogan," Eilian said, "that was told before this time of trouble began. It foretold the fading of Faerie, both in Dunlogan and Kinrowan and all the new haunts of our people here in Liomauch Og; warned as well of how the Host would grow stronger in turn. When that time came, there a new Jack would arrive in one of the Seelie Courts, come to cast down the giants as the Jacks have of old."

"I'm not a Jack," Jacky said. "I'm a girl."

Eilian nodded. "Most assuredly, yet the spirits of the Jacks of old is in you. It's a lucky name—as the tales that your people still tell can vouch for."

"I've heard that before," Arkan said. "But where do you fit in?"

"I'm the third son of a third son of—"

"A third son," Arkan finished. "I see."

"Well, I don't," Kate said.

"It's like in the stories, isn't it?" Jacky asked.

Eilian nodded again. "The histories of Faerie tend to repeat themselves as much as your own do."

"You see," Jacky said, turning to Kate to explain it. "It's always the youngest son—not the eldest or the middle, but the third, the youngest son, that wins through in the end. It's in all the stories."

"Why?"

"Oh, Kate. I don't know. Because that's the way it works."

"But this isn't a story."

"It might as well be one." Jacky grinned. "Hobs and giants and bogans and all. It makes me feel light-headed."

"I shouldn't wonder. You've lost about ten pounds of hair."

Jacky turned to her reflection, lifting a hand to the blonde stubble. "Oh, God! Look at me! I'd forgotten how terrible I looked."

"That's the least of our problems," Kate said.

"That's easy for you to say."

"I just did."

Jacky tried out a fierce look on Kate but couldn't hold it. The two erupted in laughter leaving Eilian and Arkan shaking their heads. Arkan turned to the Laird's son. "I think it's something about the air of Faerie," he said. "Even in a place like this."

"Either that," Eilian said, "or mortals *are* all mad."

Jacky finally caught her breath. "You were saying?" she prompted.

"Times have been bad," Eilian said after a moment or two, "and getting worse. When word came north of how Gyre the Elder was moving his Court into Kinrowan, our Billy Blind said it was time now for me to go and help as I could. Three knots he tied in my hair, one for each—"

"What's a Billy Blind?" Jacky asked, interrupting.

Arkan replied. "It's a custom we brought with us from the old country. Every Court has one—a man or woman who has been crippled or blinded. They can often see into the days to come and the old magics run strong in them—as recompense, some say. Even your folk had them in the old days."

Jacky's mouth shaped a small "O." Then she turned to Eilian. "And he tied knots in your hair?"

Eilian nodded. "One for each mortal danger I must face. Here, look." He turned his head so that Jacky could see two small braided knots of hair that hung behind his right ear.

"There's only two."

Eilian nodded again, adding a smile. "That's because one's come undone—after you rescued me from the Unseelie Court this evening."

"You mean you've got to go through that two more times?"

"That . . . or something like it."

"Oh." The prospect wasn't very pleasing to Jacky. "Well, at least you know you'll be okay, won't you? I mean, something'll happen, and you'll pull through until both those knots are gone as well—right?"

"It's not that assured, unfortunately," Eilian replied.

"It's usually that way with augurings," Arkan added.

"Easy for you to say," Kate said, "seeing how you don't have knots in your hair."

Arkan smiled. "How do you know what I do or do not have in my hair?"

"The thing we've got to do," Jacky said, "is get out of here." She didn't like all this talk about hair and who had what in theirs. "I say we make our way to the Gruagagh's Tower and stay there tonight, then head out for Calabogie first thing in the morning."

"And the Hunt?" Arkan asked.

"I've got a plan."

Kate looked at Jacky and shook her head. "I don't think I'm going to like this at all," she said.

Over Kate's protests, Jacky took her jacket and went to the washroom. Moments later the door opened and Kate saw her friend come out, but knew that no one else would, for she was wearing the blue jacket now, with its hob-spelled stitcheries. She frowned at Arkan and Eilian, neither of whom had objected to Jacky's plan because they were both enamoured with the fact that she was "the Jack, after all. She killed a giant, didn't she?"

Jacky waited by the door until a customer was leaving, then winked at Kate and slipped out behind him. It took all of Kate's willpower not to stare out the window and watch Jacky's progress. Jacky might be invisible to the Hunt, but if Kate and her two faerie companions had their noses pressed up to the window, the riders would soon know that something was up.

Count to a hundred, Jacky had said. Staring daggers at the two faerie in the booth with her who had let Jacky go through with her plan, Kate began to count.

Once she was outside, Jacky's confidence, fueled by Eilian and Arkan's admiring agreement to her plan, began to falter. There were too many shadows around her. The wind rustled leaves and the odd bit of refuse up and down the street, effectively swallowing any tell-tale sounds that might have warned her of approaching bogans and the like.

A car pulled into the Dairy Queen's parking lot, almost running her down. She was about to shout something at the foolidiotjerk, then realized that the poor sod behind the wheel couldn't have seen her. Not with the jacket on. She glanced back at the restaurant where Kate and the others were playing their part. Then, biting at her lower lip, she faced the three riders of the Hunt across the street from her.

This, she realized, might not be one of her brightest ideas. But it was too late to back out now. They had to do something. It was that, or dawdle around the old DQ until the place closed and they were kicked out. By then who knew how many of the Unseelie Court would be skulking around, looking for tasty mortals to gnaw on.

She shivered, remembering her helplessness in the Civic Centre. But you got away, she told herself. And you did kill a giant. They'll be scared of *you* now. Right. Sure.

She started across the street.

Fifty-five, fifty-six.
Surely she could dare a peek?
Fifty-seven, fifty-eight.
Kate's nerves were all jangling. She should have insisted that she be the one to go out. At least then she wouldn't be stuck inside here worrying.
Sixty, sixty-one.
She glanced casually out the window, saw Jacky starting across the street, then just as casually stretched and looked back at her companions.
"I wonder what's taking her so long in there," she said to Arkan who obligingly turned and looked at the door to the washroom.
Sixty-nine, seventy.
He shrugged as he looked back at her. "Maybe she's looking for knots in her hair," he said.
Eilian and Kate laughed.
Seventy-four.
Kate wondered if Eilian's laugh sounded as hollow to him as hers did to her.
Seventy-six.
If I was a Huntsman, she thought, I'd *know* something was up, just by the way we're all sitting in this booth like a bunch of geeks.
Eighty, eighty-one.

• • •

As she passed by the Hunt, Jacky was tempted to grab
something and whack one of them over the head, but all she
did was go by as softly as she could, positive that they could
hear her knees rattling against each other, her teeth chattering, her pulse drumming out: "HereIam, hereIam!" And
then, just when she was as close to them as her path would
take her, one of them lifted his head and looked around himself uneasily.

Oh, shit, Jacky thought.

Close as she was, she could see that the impression of
emptiness under their helmets was caused by visors of non-
reflective dark plexiglas. The one who had lifted his head now
pushed back his visor and for the first time Jacky got a glimpse
at what a Huntsman really looked like. His features surprised
her. He seemed quite human—rough and craggy, but human
all the same. He didn't have anything like the monstrous vis-
age she'd imagined. Of course the way he looked wasn't going to stop him from giving the alarm once he spotted her.
His gaze settled on where she was standing.

This is it, she thought. I'm doomed.

But then a truck went by on the street and she moved
quickly with it, hob-stitched sneakers lending her the necessary speed, the truck's passage swallowing any sound she
might make. When she reached the position in front of the
Bingo Hall that she'd been making for, she looked back to
see that the rider had dropped his visor once more, his attention turned elsewhere. Jacky glanced over at the Dairy Queen.

She hadn't been counting herself, so she wasn't sure how long
she had to wait. Just a couple of secs, she thought, but time
dragged. She peeked back down the sidewalk at the three riders.
She could tell just by looking at them that they knew something
was about to happen, they just didn't know what.

Hang in there, fellas, she thought. The show's about to
start.

She wondered why she was so thirsty. Her throat felt like
somebody had rubbed it with sandpaper. Come *on*, Kate.
How long can it take to get to—

A hundred.

This is it, Kate thought. She got up and knocked on the

door of the washroom while Arkan went outside to the car. Eilian stood by the door waiting for her. She knocked again, looked across the street to see the riders moving to their bikes, then glanced at Arkan. His head was under the dashboard looking for the ignition wires. When Judith coughed into life, he sat up and grinned at them, then tromped on the gas. The VW leapt across the parking lot with a squeal of tires.

Jacky waited, her coat unbuttoned, until the VW started. Then she pulled off the jacket and stepped out from under the awning of the Bingo Hall and onto the pavement.

"Hey, bozos!" she cried.

The riders, moving for their Harleys, paused at the sound of her voice. She couldn't see the surprise register on their faces because of their dark plexiglas visors, but their indecision was plain in their body language.

Do it! she willed to Arkan.

At that moment the VW came tearing out of the parking lot. Jacky moved towards the riders, but slowly, making them hesitate. Then Arkan was aiming Judith at their bikes.

He hit the brakes as he neared the big choppers and the car slewed sideways. It hit the first bike and sent it crashing into the others. The riders leapt out of the way as the three machines toppled. Arkan brought Judith to an abrupt halt, backed up, popped the clutch back into first. The transmission shrieked. He floored the gas again, driving the bikes against one another and up against a streetlamp. Jacky didn't stay to watch any more.

She ran across the street for the front door of the Dairy Queen where Kate and Eilian were waiting. They watched Arkan back Judith away from the bikes and roar across the street to where they waited. The fenders and front trunk of the little car were a mess—crushed in, bumper hanging askew, one headlight dangling from the left side, the other shining straight up into the sky on the right.

"My car!" Kate wailed. "It's ruined!"

Arkan pulled to a screeching stop and Eilian opened the passenger's door. Grabbing Kate's arm, Jacky propelled her into the car. They both got into the back—Kate under protest.

Eilian was half in when Arkan pulled away. He turned left at Riverdale, moving quickly through the gears up to third.

"It worked!" Jacky cried. She twisted around, peering out the back window. She could see the riders trying to untangle their machines. "We've lost them."

"I've had this car for seven years," Kate said.

"We'll get you another one," Jacky told her.

"You can't buy these anymore—not like Judith." She glared at Jacky. "How could you do this to Judith?"

"I . . ." It had been such a good plan, Jacky thought. And it had worked too. But she'd never really thought about what it would do to Kate's car. "Jeez, Kate. I wasn't trying to wreck her."

"God! Imagine if you had been."

"Well, you're the one who insisted on coming along."

"I . . ." Now it was Kate's turn to deflate. "I suppose I did. It's just that . . ."

Jacky gave her a hug. "We'll get her fixed up," she promised. "We'll make the Gruagagh put a spell on her."

"Do you think he would?"

"Your chance to ask him is coming right up," Arkan said from the front seat as he pulled into the driveway beside the house that was the Gruagagh's Tower.

The front yard was all overgrown as well, though not so badly as the back. A tall oak stood sentinel on the lawn, branches bare of leaves spreading overhead. A rundown garage, its door closed and the whole structure leaning a bit to one side, crouched at the end of the driveway. The house was dark. It looked, at that moment, more deserted than ever.

"End of the line," Arkan said.

Eilian got out first. As Jacky and Kate disembarked, he opened the garage door. There was plenty of room inside, so Arkan drove Judith in, then reached down and undid the wires, killing the engine. Eilian closed the garage door behind Arkan and they rejoined Jacky and Kate.

"Jeez," Jacky said, looking at the dark house.

Second and third thoughts were busily cluttering up her mind. Her stupid throat had gone all dry again. She swallowed with a grimace.

"I hope he's in a good mood," she said as she led the way to the front door and knocked.

CHAPTER
14

When subsequent knocking, and even a few well-placed kicks against the Gruagagh's door elicited no response, Jacky tried the doorknob. To her surprise, it turned easily under her hand and the door swung open. Shadows fled down the hallway, banished by the vague illumination of the streetlights behind her. But some of them seemed to move in the wrong direction. For a moment she thought she saw a coatrack against the wall by the door, but as soon as she looked at it, it was gone. There were vague sounds, creakings and stirrings that seemed more than just an old house settling in on itself.

She could remember Bhruic telling her that this was the best protected place in the Laird's lands. Oh, really? Then how come it was so easy to get in?

"Bhruic?" she called down the hallway. It was still filled with shadows, but now they lay motionless. The creaks and stirring quieted. "Are you there, Bhruic?"

Her voice echoed through the house. The stillness that followed was absolute. A horrible feeling began to rise in her. She remembered her first visit here. It was hard to forget the tall, forbidding Gruagagh, the sly movements spied in the shadows and the ghostly furniture that never really seemed to be there when you looked straight at it. She started forward, but a quick brown hand closed its fingers around her arm and hauled her back.

116

"You *never* go unbidden into a Gruagagh's Tower," Arkan warned.

"I don't think he's here anymore," Jacky said, shaking her arm free.

"He has to be," Kate said.

Jacky's bad feeling grew more pronounced. Something was definitely wrong here. Either the Unseelie Court had found a way to breach Bhruic's defenses or . . . or he had left on his own. Either way, she felt betrayed.

"I'm going in," she said. "Whoever wants to can wait out here, but I'm going in."

She moved into the hallway and this time no one tried to stop her. Kate hesitated, then followed with Eilian. Arkan stood uncertainly on the stoop. He looked back at the deserted street, cars parked in neat rows along one side, houses spilling rectangularly-shaped yellow lights from their windows onto their lawns. Swallowing once, he faced the Tower again and went inside.

A feeling of certain doom made his chest go tight as he crossed the threshold and he found it hard to breathe. His faerie senses could see deeper into the shadows, could hear far more clearly. There was a feeling of *otherness* all about him. But as he closed the door and followed the others down the hall, and still nothing happened—no lightning bolts, no angry Gruagagh roaring at them—his initial fears quieted a little. But only to make room for new ones.

If the Gruagagh *wasn't* here, what hope was left for them? The Gruagagh held the heart of the Laird's kingdom in trust. If he had betrayed them . . . The rumours that had abounded when the Unseelie Court stole away the Laird's daughter returned to haunt him. Oh, moon and stars! If the Gruagagh was in league with the Host . . .

"Where could he be?" Jacky whispered. "He promised— promised!—me he couldn't leave the Tower."

"Maybe he doesn't know we're here," Eilian said. "He could be upstairs, out of earshot . . ."

"Look," Kate said.

She was standing by an open doorway, pointing in. The others joined her. They could see Windsor Park through the room's windows. Phantom furniture came and went as they looked about, then the room appeared to be empty, except for a small figure lying on a huddle of blankets in a corner.

"It's Finn," Jacky said, crossing the room.

She knelt by the little man and touched his shoulder. His eyelids fluttered at her touch. His eyes opened to look, first at her, then over her shoulder where Kate and the other two members of their small company stood.

"Where . . . where am I?" he asked.

"In the Tower," Jacky said.

The little man's features blanched. "The . . . the Gruagagh's Tower?"

Jacky nodded. "Where is he, Finn?"

"Where . . . ?" The hob sat up, a hand rising to rub at his temple. "The last thing I remember is the bogans grabbing you and then something hitting me harder than I ever care to be hit again . . ." His voice trailed off as his fingers explored his scalp. "At least I thought I was hit on the head. But there's not even a bump."

"The Gruagagh fixed you up," Kate said.

"And now he's gone," Jacky added, trying to keep the hurt from her voice.

Why did he lie to her? Finding Finn here, alive and unhurt, proved that the Host hadn't stormed the place. So where could the Gruagagh have gone? And why?

"I'm going to look around some more," she said. "Kate, can you show me that room upstairs?"

Kate nodded, but it was Arkan who spoke.

"We should go," he said. "It's bad enough we're in his Tower without his leave; it'll be worse if we go poking and prying."

"The Gruagagh is gone?" Finn asked. "And you're spying on him? Jacky Rowan, are you mad?"

"Angry, maybe, but not the kind of mad you mean. Come on, Kate."

The two women left the room with Eilian and began to explore the other rooms. "This is bad," they could hear Finn mutter behind them as they started up the stairs. "This is very bad."

The halls and rooms upstairs were all dark, free of dust and unfurnished, and there was no one there. There were no ghostly furnishings anymore, no sense of sly movement in the deeper shadows. Jacky had an eerie feeling moving through the deserted house. She felt like a ghost, like she didn't belong here or anywhere anymore. With the Gruagagh's disappearance she had to wonder how much of anything that he'd told her was true.

Why did he want her to go to the Giants' Keep? What if Lorana wasn't there? Or if she was already dead? If he was in league with the Unseelie Court, he might have been setting her and Kate up for . . . well, God knew what. When she thought of the bogans and their prodding fingers, the hunger in their eyes . . . She didn't plan to end up in a stew, that much was certain.

"I can't find it," Kate said.

They were on the third floor now and had been in and out of every room at least a half dozen times.

"A room can't just disappear," Jacky said.

"A gruagagh's can," Eilian said. "Our Billy Blind has places he can sit and never the one of us can see or find him until he suddenly steps out—as if from nowhere."

"A Billy Blind's like a gruagagh, isn't he?" Jacky asked.

"Sort of a poor man's gruagagh?"

Eilian nodded. "My father's Court is not so big as some—not so big as Kinrowan, that's for certain. And we have no gruagagh to spell the Samhaine charms—only a Billy Blind."

"Well, what do you do on Samhaine Eve then?"

"Hide and hope."

"Hide and hope," Jacky repeated. She looked around the third floor landing where they were standing. "Can you hear me, Bhruic Dearg? Are you hiding somewhere near? Well, come out and talk to us, dammit!" She stamped her foot on the wooden floor, but its echoes were the only sound that replied. "Was everything he told me a lie?" she asked no one in particular.

Eilian shook his head. "There *is* a Horn that rules the Hunt and the Laird of Kinrowan's daughter *was* stolen by the Unseelie Court—those weren't lies. And you, Jacky. You are the only Jack we have now."

"I wish you'd stop calling me that. I'm a woman. You make me sound like a sailor."

"It's a title," Eilian said. "Like 'Billy Blind.' Our Billy Blind's not named Billy, nor even William."

She forced a small smile to her lips. "I guess we might as well go back downstairs. Do you think this place'll be safe enough for us tonight? I don't see us going to Calabogie tonight, but the way we all just waltzed in here . . . I don't know."

"So we're still going?" Kate asked.

"What else can we do?" she asked. "With or without the Gruagagh, we've still got the Host to contend with. The only idea worth following through on is the one we started out with—get the Horn and use it to find and free Lorana. The Laird's folk will rally around her and, if we've got the Horn, then we control the Hunt. After we use it to find Lorana, we can turn the Hunt on the Unseelie Court and see how they like being on the receiving end for a change."

"This is still a gruagagh's Tower," Eilian said. "I think we'll be safe here—from Gyre the Elder's people at any rate. But if the Gruagagh returns and decides he doesn't care to guest us . . ."

"If the Gruagagh shows up," Jacky said, "he'll be too busy answering a question or two that I've got for him to be bothering anyone. Believe me."

"Getting real fierce, are we?" Kate said to her as they started down the stairs.

"Oh, jeez, Kate. Am I getting too weird?"

Kate shook her head. "With bogans and gruagaghs and men that turn into swans running around? I don't think so, kid. It's about time you got a little fierce."

Jacky sighed. "Can you just see Will's face if he could see us now? And he thought I was too predictable."

"Maybe we should stop by his place tonight," Kate said with a grin. "We can see how he likes standing off a bunch of bogans for us while we get a little sleep."

"Oh, wouldn't I just!"

"Who's Will?" Eilian asked.

Jacky glanced at him. "Just somebody I never knew," she said.

Very fierce, Kate thought approvingly. Whatever else this madcap affair left them, at least it had finally brought Jacky out of her shell. Not that Kate had ever agreed with Will. His

idea of bar-and-party-hopping as the means to having a ful-
filled life wasn't exactly her concept of what Jacky had
needed. All Jacky had needed was some confidence in herself. With some confidence, Kate knew Jacky could do anything. And she was proving it now.

CHAPTER
15

When Kate left him, her recriminations still ringing in his ears, the Gruagagh of Kinrowan returned to the third floor room with its view of the city in miniature. He marked the various positions of the riders of the Hunt, the gathering of bogans and hags, gullywudes, trolls and other creatures of the Unseelie Court. Of the Laird's folk there were few and, of those few he could see, all save the odd forester were hiding.

Not so the Host.

As night fell, he watched the sluagh rise from their marshy beds. The trolls under their bridges grew bolder. Packs of gullywudes and spriggans and other unwholesome, if minor, members of the Unseelie Court ran up and down the city streets, chasing leaves and the pets of humans, and sometimes humans as well. They never showed themselves. Instead they teased with fingers like wind and voices like wind, awaking fears that didn't settle even when the humans were safe within their homes and the doors closed on the eerie night.

He could not see into the building where the bogans held Jacky captive, but he could imagine what went on in there. The greedy faces pressed close to her, feeding on her fear as much as the smell of her. If the giants didn't want her for their own, the stew pots would already be heating. She would be despairing . . .

"Use your wits, woman," he whispered into the night.
"Why do you think the powers that be gave them to you, if
not to use?"

But then he saw the new captive that the Host brought into
the building. The swan wings would have told anyone what
the new captive was, but even without them Bhruic would
have known. He had not served Lairdsfolk for so long as he
had without recognizing them; by sight, by sound, by smell,
no matter what shape they wore. He recognized who this
young Lairdling was, too. Dunlogan's son. His third son.
Eilian. The Giants' Keep would ring with celebrations tonight. A new Lairdling to add to their bestiary, and a Jack as
well.

He closed his eyes, not to shut away the sight of what lay
in front of him, but to seek council inside. He let his inner
turmoil rise and fret, caught each fear and loosed it from
inside him like so many freed birds until only silence lay
there, deep and soothing. And filled with possibilities. They
lay like threads in front of his closed eyes, going every-which-
way, unravelling into pasts and presents and times yet to
come. He couldn't work them, couldn't weave them, that was
for other hands more skilled than his, but he could take one
thread, one possibility, and tie his need to it, then send it
forth from his silence like a summoning call.

For a long time he stood by the window, motionless, sightless as Eilian's Billy Blind, which was to say he saw not the
world around him, but the worlds within. He stood and
waited, without expectations, but open to what might come;
not hoping, but neither did he feel hopeless. And the first
inkling he had that his call was answered was a sound that
appeared to rise up from inside him, it seemed so close. A
rhythm like hooves drumming on long hills, a winding call
like a horn sounding, a melody that was fiddling, piping,
harping—all at once.

"I hear you, Gruagagh," a voice said softly. "Has the
time come for you to set aside your spells and come with me
for good?"

Bhruic opened his eyes. Before him, lounging on the windowsill, was a slender man who wore trousers and a jacket
that looked to be made of heather and twigs and leaves all
woven together; whose feet were unshod for they were hooves;

whose red-gold hair fell in curls around an old-young face;
whose eyes were too dark and too deep and too wise to be
the eyes of mortal or faerie. He held a fiddle loosely in the
crook of his arm, an instrument of polished wood with a head
carved into the semblance of a stag's. He reached out and
tapped Bhruic with the end of his bow.

"Well?" he asked.

Bhruic shook his head. "I need a small favour."

The stranger smiled. "I doubt it's that simple."

"It never is," Bhruic agreed.

"You play your hand too much in shadow," the stranger
said. "But you know that already, don't you?"

The fiddle went up under his chin and the bow licked across
its strings. The melody he played was both merry and sad
and he didn't play it for long. When he was done, he studied
Bhruic for a time.

"You were a poet first," he said finally. "A bard. You
could have been the best poet we had. Do you still remember
what it was like before you let wizardry rule your life?"

"There was no one else to do what needed to be done.
Kinrowan had no gruagagh."

"And were you truly the man for the task? Will all the
music and song you never played or wrote be worth it?"

Bhruic made no reply.

Kerevan smiled. "So be it. What small favour do you need,
Gruagagh of Kinrowan? And ask me not again to look for
the Laird's daughter you lost, for you know I can't."

"It's the one called Jacky Rowan," Bhruic said.

A fiddle string rang out as Kerevan plucked it. "Ah," he
said. "That one."

He leaned back so that the Gruagagh could look out the
window. Bhruic saw the tiny figures of Jacky and Eilian in
the parking lot of Lansdowne Park, surrounded by bogans
and gullywudes, saw Kate's Volkswagen pulling in off Bank
Street.

"But the giant . . . ?"

"She killed it. She's a Rowan and Jack—haven't you said
so yourself? What she doesn't win through pluck, she wins
through luck. That was always the way with Jacks—even in
the old days. She'll be cannier than even she knows herself,
that one."

"It's still a long road to the Giants' Keep."

Kerevan nodded. "That it is. And a great deal can happen to one upon that road these days, if you take my meaning," he added with a sly wink. Then he frowned. "You shouldn't meddle with the Host, Bhruic. Nor with the Laird's Court either. Our kind were not meant to strike bargains with either—you know that."

"Do I have a choice?" Bhruic asked.

"You always have a choice—no matter who you bargain with. But speaking of bargains, what will ours be? What's its worth? Will you go with me?"

Silence lay between them as Bhruic hesitated. Then finally he sighed.

"On Samhaine day," he said. "If all goes well."

"On Samhaine day no matter how it goes," Kerevan returned.

Bhruic hesitated again.

"Don't you trust your luck?" Kerevan asked.

"On Samhaine day," Bhruic agreed.

"Done!"

Up went the fiddle again, under Kerevan's chin, and down went the bow. The tune that spilled forth was a mixture of three or four reels that he tumbled together willy-nilly, but with great feeling. Laying aside the bow, he grinned.

"But mind," he said. "You're not to talk to Host or Seelie Court till my return—I'll not have you making new bargains on top of the one we have ourselves."

Bhruic nodded.

"Now what's this small favour you'd have in return?" Kerevan asked.

The Gruagagh sat beside him on the windowsill. "This is what I'd have you do," he said.

When they were done making bargains, Kerevan picked up his fiddle again. Hopping about on his cloven hooves, he sawed away at his fiddle until the room rang with the sound of his music. Bhruic could feel his own blood quicken.

"Until Samhaine, Kerevan," he said.

He closed his eyes. The threads were there once more, moving and weaving in time to Kerevan's reels. Bhruic unravelled the one that had brought the fiddler. The music faded and when he opened his eyes he was alone once more.

He meditated for a long time in that room that looked out on more views than it should. When he heard Jacky and her companions arrive, he spoke the necessary words that would hide him and the room from any but another gruagagh's sight, in the same way that a Billy Blind will speak a word and sit unnoticed in a corner of his Laird's hearth, forever and a day if that was what he wished. Bhruic meant to keep his side of the bargain, just as he knew Kerevan, capable of mischief as he was, would keep his.

He heard Jacky and Kate and the Laird of Dunlogan's son stomping about on the third floor, looking for him, looking for this room, but the sounds came as though from a great distance. When he gazed out the window once more, the grand view of Ottawa was gone.

In place of the panorama of the Laird's holdings, he saw only the street below. There were gullywudes down there, sniffing and creeping about on twig-thin limbs. Bogans, sluagh, and a troll too. At the far end of the street, a Huntsman sat astride his motorcycle, featureless in the shadows that cloaked him from all eyes but those of faerie. Then he saw Kerevan wandering down below as well, fiddle under his chin and playing a tune.

The music of Kerevan's fiddle drove them all away. The gullywudes scurried away and hid. The bogans snarled and made threatening gestures, but they too finally retreated. The sluagh hissed and whispered, faded like mist. Last to go was the troll, snuffling as he wandered aimlessly down the street, hitting the concrete with a big wooden club as he went. A forester from the Laird's Court happened by then, but he too was sent off by the spell in the fiddler's music.

Then only Kerevan was there, hooves clicking, fiddle playing. And the rider. Motionless in his shadows. And that was the way it remained for the rest of the night.

CHAPTER
16

"I dreamt I heard a fiddle play—all night long," Jacky said when she woke the next morning.

They had slept in the room overlooking Windsor Park, the five of them sharing the blankets that the Gruagagh had left for Finn, the hard wooden floor for their mattress. They woke in various moods of discomfort. Finn and Arkan were nervous about their surroundings. Kate hadn't appreciated the meager sleeping arrangements and felt a bit grumpy, while Jacky was still fuming about the Gruagagh's disappearance. Only Filian was cheerful.

"I heard it too," he said. "And I thought I knew that music—or at least who played it—but it's not so clear now that the sun's up and I'm more awake."

"Unseelie musicians, that's who played outside this Tower last night," Finn said. "Who else would be abroad in Kinrowan? Only the Unseelie Court . . . and gruagaghs. Oh, we're in for a bad time, I just know it."

"The Host has gruagaghs too?" Jacky asked.

"Every court has wizards of one sort or another," Arkan said. "Even your own folk."

"Can't trust them either," Finn added. "Not one of them. And the Gruagagh of Kinrowan himself is in league with Moon knows what."

"He fixed you up," Kate pointed out.

"For what?" Finn asked. "For why? No good'll come of it—mark my words."

Jacky looked away from the window. She'd been standing there, watching the sunlight fill the park. She felt better now, with the night gone. She hadn't just heard music last night. She'd heard the whispering sound of sluagh around the Tower, the restless dead calling out in their mournful voices. Not close, not as close as the fiddling, but too close for comfort.

"We'll just have to make our own good," she said. "And we'll start by going to Calabogie. Now, while the sun's up and the Host's not so strong. Unless anyone's got any better suggestions?"

Kate looked up from where she sat, cleaning her nails with her little Swiss penknife. "Breakfast?" she tried.

"We can stop for it along the way."

"I'm ready to go," Eilian said and one by one the others nodded, even Finn.

"Don't we make a grand company," the hob muttered as they followed Jacky to the front of the house. "We've got Gyre and all his kin just shaking in their boots, I'm sure."

"She did kill a giant," Arkan said, nodding ahead to Jacky.

"There's that," Finn agreed.

Jacky had reached the front door and flung it open. Standing on the steps, arms akimbo, she looked up and down the street. October sun was bright in the crisp air. The grey pavement of the sidewalks and streets was ablaze with the colour of dried leaves that scurried and spun down their lengths. With her redcap on, though she didn't really need it anymore, Jacky studied every possible hiding place, and a few more besides, but could see nothing. Not anything dangerous. Not anything at all. They could easily be alone in the world, the street was that quiet.

"They're not here," Arkan said wonderingly. "I knew we could lose the Hunt for a while, but I thought sure they'd have tracked us down by now. Yet there's not a soul to be seen."

Jacky nodded, though she still sensed something watching them. She couldn't spot whatever it was. "It'll be a tight squeeze—five of us in Judith," she said to Kate.

"I'm *still* going," Kate said.

"Of course you are. I'm just saying it's going to be cramped, that's all."

"Kerevan," Arkan said suddenly.

Jacky gave him a strange look. "What?"

"Last night—the fiddling you heard. It was Kerevan playing."

"Who or what is Kerevan?" Kate asked.

"No one's all that sure," Finn explained. "There's some say he was here when the first faerie arrived, others say he's of mixed blood—that of Kinrowan and that of the native faerie."

Eilian nodded. "That's right. I've heard that story. And he's mostly seen in Kinrowan's lands—if he's seen at all. But that hasn't been for many years."

"What does it matter?" Jacky asked.

"Well, before the Gruagagh of Kinrowan became the Gruagagh, he was prenticed as a bard. He went into the Borderlands between Kinrowan and Dunlogan and prenticed himself to Kerevan, who learned his own craft from the old Bucca, Salamon Brien. There was a great to-do about it—especially in those days when we didn't have the Host to worry about so much—because the Bucca's one of the fiaina sidhe, you see, those faerie who bow to no Laird."

Finn nodded in agreement with what Eilian was saying. "There's always been a strain of something strange following the Gruagagh of Kinrowan," he said. "If it's not prenticing himself to Kerevan, it's becoming the Gruagagh in the first place. If it's not being the best of both—poet and wizard— it's losing the Laird's daughter to Gyre the Elder and suffering no more than a few hurts himself."

"But what's *wrong* with this Kerevan?" Kate asked.

"Why he's dead," Arkan said. "He's been dead for a hundred and fifty years."

"So it was his ghost we heard last night . . ?"

"Oh, great," Jacky said. "That's all we need. I think it's time we hopped to it. We can exchange all the ghostly stories you want on the drive up, but let's get going."

She led the way to the garage, as she'd led the way out of the Gruagagh's Tower. Taking the lead was coming naturally to her—which was odd enough in its way, she thought. But odder still was the way the others were deferring to her. It came, she supposed, from killing giants. This morning she didn't feel weird about that. It was as though she'd seen an exciting, if a little bit overly gruesome, movie the night before and, while she could remember what had happened, the gory details weren't so clear anymore.

Arkan lifted the garage door and they all stared at the car.

"Judith!" Kate cried. "Look at her!"

"She's never going to make it," Jacky said.

"Oh, we'll get her running," Arkan said.

With Eilian's help, and Kate fussing about over their shoulders like a concerned mother, Arkan managed to bang the VW's fenders into a semblance of their proper shape. A piece of wire pulled taut around each of the lights had them pointing straight again. The dent in the bumper they banged out with a rock from the Gruagagh's garden.

"Well, what do you think?" Arkan asked, finally, stepping back to admire his own handiwork.

"We'll get her fixed up properly as soon as we're back," Jacky promised, cutting Kate off in the middle of a rant about what exactly was wrong, everything was wrong, were they blind that they couldn't see that poor Judith was just so much junk now thanks to . . .

Jacky squeezed into the back with Kate and Finn. Eilian and Arkan rode up front with Arkan driving. The car started smoothly as Arkan connected the ignition wires. He backed out of the garage and onto the street at a reasonable speed that bore no resemblance to last's night flamboyant ride. Jacky peered out the back window and all around as they drove off but, while the feeling of being watched persisted—they *were* being watched—she couldn't see by whom, or from where. Then they were on Riverdale. The Gruagagh's street was left behind, and with it, the feeling.

Hobs weren't the only beings that could stitch invisibility. Hidden through the Hunt's special magics, one of the nine riders watched and waited. As soon as the VW started up in the Gruagagh's garage, the rider kick-started his Harley. He waited until the VW was almost at the end of the block, then fed the bike some gas. But before it could pull away, the music started.

It came from all around him, catching him unaware. His hands went lax on the handlebars. The bike coughed and stalled. The rider slumped in his seat and the machine began

to totter. Before it fell over, a lithe figure with cloven feet
slipped forward and leaned his own weight against the bike,
keeping it upright, all the while playing his fiddle.

The rider was firmly snared in the music's spell—something Kerevan had only accomplished by taking the rider by
surprise. It wouldn't last long. He lifted the bow from his
fiddle and slid the pair of them into the sack that hung from
his shoulder. Then he took a firmer grip on the motorcycle
and let the rider slide off it, onto the ground. He grinned
down at the fallen Huntsman as he straddled the machine.

"Oh, my," he said, kicking the Harley into life once more.
"Won't this be something."

He roared out of the rider's hiding place in time to see the
VW turn onto Riverdale. Giving a jaunty wave towards the
window where he knew the Gruagagh was watching, he fed
the bike some more gas with a relaxed twist of his wrist and
sped off in pursuit of the little car, humming a hornpipe under
his breath. The tune was "The Tailer's Twist" and most ap-
propriate it was too, he thought.

"It seems fairly straightforward," Jacky said. "We just
take the Queensway out to Highway 7, follow that to Arn-
prior, down 2 until we reach Burnstown, and then the 508 to
Calabogie."

She was reading their route from one of Kate's maps that
was a part of the clutter underfoot in the cramped back seat.

"But that's just it," Kate said. "If it's that straightforward,
won't they have some nasty surprises waiting for us along the
way?"

"The other choice is to go down to . . . oh, Perth, say,
then take Highway 1 up through Lanark to where it turns into
511—but 511's a pretty windy and hilly road. If we're looking
for good ambush country, that'd be it. What do you think,
Arkan?"

"We should take the quickest way," he replied. "There'll
be enough of the Host around the Keep by day. Come nightfall, their numbers will easily triple."

"What did the Gruagagh suggest?" Finn asked.

Jacky frowned and folded the map with a snap. "What the
Gruagagh does or doesn't suggest isn't our concern."

In the front seat, Arkan and Eilian exchanged glances.

"Remind me never to get on her bad side," Arkan said in a loud stage whisper.

Jacky gave him a playful whack on the shoulder with the map. "I heard that," she told him.

Leaning forward, she turned on Judith's radio, switching stations until one came on playing the Montreal group Luba's latest single, "Let It Go."

"I like this one," she said with a smile.

She turned up the volume and squeezed back in between Kate and Finn as the lively song with its hint of a Caribbean dance beat filled the car with an infectious rhythm.

They reached the turn-off to Pakenham without incident, having decided to leave the main highway once they'd covered half the distance to Calabogie. The radio had long since been turned off, though Jacky was still singing "Let It Go" under her breath. The bridge in Pakenham was under construction and they had to wait a few minutes before their lane could move. The Mississippi River was on their right, bearing no resemblance to its American cousin except for its name. On the left was a big stone building that had been built in 1840 as a private home, but now housed Andrew Dickson's—a well-known craft and artisan gallery.

"I had a friend who had a showing there," Jacky said. "Remember Judy Shaw?"

Kate nodded.

"I have a cousin who lived there for a while," Finn remarked. "But he had to move because of Grump Kow."

"Now who's Grump Kow?" Kate asked.

"The troll who lives under this bridge they're working on."

"Lovely. I had to ask."

Their lane was clear now and Arkan steered across the bridge. He followed the road into Pakenham, then turned right onto 15. It turned into 23 before they hit White Lake, then they took Highway 2 into Burnstown.

"I'm starving!" Jacky said and insisted they stop at the Burnstown General Store.

It was an old brick building and, in honour of the approaching Halloween, had pumpkins lining the concrete steps leading up to the front door, and a straw man in wellie boots, jeans and a plaid shirt tied to one of the porch supports. They filled up on coffee, sandwiches and donuts, sitting on the porch while they ate.

"So far we're clear," Arkan said. "I'm not sure if that makes me feel good or not."

"Doesn't it mean that we've lost them for sure?" Kate asked.

"Not really. They know where we're going. I'm afraid the reason we're being left alone now is because they're preparing something really horrible for us in Calabogie."

Finn stared at his half-eaten donut. "All of a sudden, I'm not hungry anymore."

"Time we were going anyway," Jacky said with false jollity.

"Easy for you to say—you've already finished eating."

"Don't mind her, Finn," Kate said. "She's feeling terribly fierce these days."

Eilian laughed as he gathered up their wrappers and empty coffee cups and dumped them in a garbage barrel at the end of the porch.

"All aboard!" Arkan called.

They piled back into the VW, Jacky leaning into the front seats again as she tried to see just what it was that Arkan did with the wires to make the car start without a key. Judith coughed into life without Jacky being any the wiser as to exactly how it had been managed, and then they were off again, taking 508 on the last leg of their journey to Calabogie.

Cloaked in a spell that hid him far better than either a hob's stitcheries or a Huntsman's magics, Kerevan kicked his borrowed Harley into life and followed after them once more.

The lack of pursuit or any interest by way of the Host troubled him as well. He was of half a mind to speed ahead and spy out what lay in wait, but didn't dare risk letting the VW out of sight. If something happened to his charge while he was spying ahead, his bargain with Bhruic would be voided. And that he wouldn't allow. He'd waited long enough for Bhruic to shed his Gruagagh cloak. Too long, by any reckoning.

But he had a bad feeling about what lay ahead.

• • •

Calabogie, which was first settled in the early 1800s, could be considered the hub of Bagot & Blythfield Township. The Township takes up an area of 175.9 square miles, two thirds of which is Crown Land. Calabogie has a resident population of 1600 that swells to over 4000 in the summer when the cottagers descend upon it. The town takes its name from the Gaelic word "Calaboyd," meaning "marshy shore," of which Calabogie Lake, on which the village is situated, has plenty.

Jacky and her friends approached it from the east. Their first inkling that they were near was when they spied Munford's Restaurant & Gas Bar, on the corner of 508 and Mill Street. Behind the restaurant was a small trailer camp.

"Where to now?" Arkan asked, slowing down.

"We go straight," Jacky said, consulting her map, "until we see a gravel pit on our right, then we turn left on a sideroad."

"Are you sure you know where we're going?" Kate asked.

Jacky pointed to her roadmap. "This is the same as the one Bhruic showed me, except it's got names we can understand instead of faerie ones. Once we hit that sideroad, we're looking for a cliff face that overlooks the lake at"—she studied the map—"McNeelys Bay."

"The cliff face is the Giants' Keep?" Eilian asked, turning around to the back seat.

Jacky nodded.

"Then perhaps we shouldn't be in quite such a hurry to drive right up to it," Eilian said. "Is there a way we can approach it from the rear?"

"Not unless you want to hike over these mountains."

"Look at that," Kate said, pointing at a motel sign as they passed it. " 'Jocko's Motel,' I love it."

Everyone looked and made suitably appreciative noises except for Arkan who was watching the rearview mirror. A pickup truck was approaching them quickly—too quickly for his liking.

"Hang on!" he cried.

"What—?" Jacky began just as the pickup rammed them from the rear, knocking them all about in the confines of the small car. Arkan fought the wheel, trying to keep Judith on the road.

"My car!" Kate moaned.

"Is that guy nuts?" Jacky cried at the same time. She turned to look out the small rear window and saw, even before Arkan called out, who was in the truck.

"Bogans is what they are!" Arkan warned.

"Can't we go any faster?" Jacky asked.

"Not with this load."

The truck rammed into them again, this time slewing them along the highway, rubber burning before Arkan managed to regain control and straighten the car. As the pickup lunged forward for a third time, Arkan hauled left on the wheel. The VW's direct steering answered with frightening efficiency. Again Judith's wheels were squealing on the concrete. Arkan tromped on the brake. The pickup, trying to correct its aim after Arkan's abrupt maneuver, went sailing by. Then its brake lights flared. There was a small bridge coming up that crossed a ravine with a creek running through it. Arkan brought the VW to a skidding stop a half dozen feet past the bridge.

"Out!" he roared. "Everybody out!"

They scrambled to obey. Arkan had his door open and was hauling Finn from the back seat. Eilian, not so quick, was on the road a half moment later, helping Kate out. Jacky saw that the pickup had stopped ahead of them. Its reverse lights went on and she knew what it was going to do—ram them again.

She froze for a long second, then Arkan had a hold of her arm and was bodily dragging her from the car. Her blue jacket, tied around her waist, caught for a moment, then came with her as she fell to the ground, half supported by Arkan. The pickup smashed into Judith and knocked the VW right off the road into the small ravine. The little car hit the rocks at the bottom with a screeching sound of buckling metal.

"We've got to run for it!" Arkan cried.

He helped Jacky to her feet, then went to get Finn who was sitting dazed by the road. The pickup was disgorging its load—three bogans from the cab, a half dozen more from its flat bed. Eilian and Kate ran to where Jacky and the others were. For a long moment they milled uncertainly, not knowing which way to run. Then the fields around them came alive with bogans and gullywudes, hags and spriggans, and an eighteen-foot-high giant who pushed his way out of a stand of small saplings to roar at them.

"Oh, Jesus," Jacky cried. "We've had it." She turned to Eilian. "Go! Fly Away! There's no sense in all of us getting caught."

Eilian hesitated.

"Do it!" she shrilled, her voice high with frustration and panic.

There was no escape for the rest of them. The ambush had been too well-planned and they'd rushed right into it like a pack of fools. Black feathers sprouted all over Eilian. Arms became wings. Neck elongated. For a brief moment there was this strange hybrid creature standing there, then the black swan lifted up into the air with an explosion of his wings. He went up, out of range of the Unseelie Court, then circled to see if he could help. The other four bunched together as the bogans encircled them.

Jacky was so mad at herself that she didn't have time to be scared. She waited for the first creature to come at her, hands curled into fists at her side. She was going to hit them and kick them and scratch them and generally make it so hard for them to tie her up that they'd regret ever coming near her. Well, at least that was her plan. Except just at that moment there came a familiar roaring sound. The throaty engine of a big chopper. A Huntsman.

The bogans hesitated in their advance. Jacky and the rest stared as one to see one of the big Harleys suddenly pop into view in the middle of the road. One moment the pavement had been empty, in the next the big machine was thundering right for them. Only the being driving it wasn't a Huntsman—or if he was, he wasn't wearing his leathers and helmet. Red-gold hair blowing, tunic fluttering and looking like so many leaves and twigs and bits of this and that sewn together, he drove right at the bogans, scattering them. His left arm reached out and snatched Jacky up, swinging her behind him, then the chopper literally leapt forward, front wheel leaving the ground as the back one burned rubber.

"No!" Jacky cried.

She didn't know if this was a friend or a foe, all she knew was that her friends were being left behind while she was speeding away. She would have jumped from the bike, but it

was going so fast she knew there was no way she'd survive
the impact when she hit the ground. She clung to the weird
rider's weirder coat.

"Please, stop!" she cried. "Those're my friends back
there. Please!"

But the stranger just drove the big bike faster.

CHAPTER
17

Kate saw the huntsman grab Jacky and speed off with her on his Harley, then the Host was swarming over them and there was no more time to worry about her friend's fate. She clawed and bit at the creatures, kicked and punched, all to no avail. The gullywudes danced out of the way of her ineffectual blows, then sidled close, tripping her, pulling at her short hair, at her clothes, pinching and striking her with sharp stick-like hands. Then the bogans had her.

They were great smelly brutes. The reek of them made her gag. The power in their hands made escape impossible. She saw Finn lose his own battle. She heard Arkan's sharp cries—like the barking and growling of a fox. He lasted the longest of the three of them, but soon he too was held captive. And then the giant was there, looming impossibly tall over them. Seeing the sheer bulk of the creature, knowing how much of Jacky's besting one of them had been luck, it still boggled her mind that her friend had been able to stand up against one, little say kill it.

All the fight went out of Finn as the giant stood over them. Arkan snarled, until a bogan cuffed him unconscious with a brutal blow. Then it was just Kate staring defiantly at him, held fast by bogans, her heart drumming in her chest. High above, Eilian soared, as helpless to help them as though he was caught himself. The giant gave a swift nod to one of the hags.

The grey naked skin of the creature seemed to swallow light as it stepped forth. It spread its arms where flaps of loose skin hung batlike between arms and torso. Two, three more hags joined the first. Up they went into the air, their take-offs awkward, but once they were airborne they moved swiftly and surely after the black swan winging high above them.

Standing near Kate, a gullywude took a sling from its belt and chose a smooth stone from the roadside. Then the sling was in motion, whirring above the little creature's head until it hummed. The gullywude released its missile and the stone went up, up, past the hags. It struck Eilian's wing and he floundered in a cloud of black feathers. Down he spiralled and Kate looked away, unwilling to see his end, but the hags caught him. Screeching like harpies, they bore him to where the Unseelie Court waited. A bogan thrust a nettle tunic roughly onto the stunned Lairdling, and then they were all captive. All helpless.

"OH," the giant boomed in good humour. "OH, HO! LOOK WHAT WE HAVE NOW! TRUSSED FOR STEW-ING, EVERY LAST ARSE-SUCKING ONE OF THEM. AND WON'T GYRE BE HAPPY WITH ME NOW, JUST WON'T HE, HOT DAMN!"

Bogans and gullywudes, hags and spriggans, all bobbed their heads in eager agreement.

"Got 'em good, Thundell," a bogan cried above the growling din of voices.

"YOU WANT A JOB DONE," the giant said, his voice carrying easily across the noise, "YOU GET A BIG MAN TO DO IT!"

Choruses of agreement followed this statement as well. The giant's huge face bent down to peer at Kate. A big finger poked at her, knocking the breath from her. The frown on that face, almost two feet wide, made her feel faint with fright.

"ARSE-BREATHING SHITHEADS!" he roared. "YOU GOT THE WRONG ONE!"

The monster's breath almost knocked Kate out. She trembled at the increased volume of his roaring voice, eardrums aching. The bogans holding her shook her fiercely as though she were to blame for Jacky's escape.

"One of the riders took her, Thundell," a reedy-voiced gullywude piped up.

"Never saw a rider like that," another muttered.

"A RIDER GOT HER? GOOD, OH, HO! GOOD! TOOK HER BACK TO GYRE, I'LL BET, HOT DAMN!" He stared around at the crowd of creatures. "WHAT ARE WE WAITING FOR, TURDBRAINS? LET'S TAKE THESE ONES IN TOO!"

Kate was dragged to the back of the pickup and dumped in the flatbed along with the other captives. So many bogans crawled on to guard them for the ride that it was hard to breathe in the crush of bodies. Gullywudes hung from the sides of the truck, danced along the top of its hood, singing shrilly, songs about stews and what went in them. The pickup started with a loud roar, lurching into motion with a grinding of gears. She was pushed against Eilian and Finn.

"Bad," she heard the little hob mutter despondently. "Oh, it's gone very bad."

She could think of nothing to add to that.

It was hard to judge how long the ride took from the ambush spot to the Giants' Keep. The smell was so bad, the cursing voices of the bogans and shrill shrieking songs of the gullywudes, the press of the bodies, all combined to make it impossible to think. Kate felt like she was in a state of shock, but knew that couldn't be completely right because she was aware of her state of mind—as though she were standing outside of herself, looking in, mind you, but aware all the same.

Arkan had recovered consciousness by the time they finally came to a halt. When the four of them were hauled from the back of the truck and thrown down to the dirt road, it was almost a relief. Leather thongs bound their arms behind them—except for Eilian who, with his swan wings and man's body, needed no such bindings—and then they began a hellish ascent up a brush-choked rise.

There were creatures ahead of them, crawling through the brush like maggots on a corpse, and more behind, pushing and shoving, laughing uproariously whenever one of the captives lost their footing, which was often. Spriggans would dart in to trip them. The stick-like gullywudes would offer their arms as branches, then pull them roughly away when

Kate or one of the others would reach for it, no longer able to tell forest growth from gullywude limb.

Beaten and weary, they were finally led in front of a great stone face near the middle of the rise. A portion of the wall swung back at their approach with a sound of grinding stone. Torches sputtered on the rock walls of the tunnel they were now pushed and dragged into. The gullywudes' various songs had fallen into one that apparently everyone knew.

> Chop in the fingers, joint by joint,
>   smell that stew, oh smell it now;
> now a tip of a nose, now the ends of the toes,
>   —better than sheep, ho! Better than a cow!

> Pop in the eyeballs, one by one,
>   smell that stew, oh smell it now . . .

The shrill voices rang in the confines of the tunnel, bouncing back from side to side until it sounded like hundreds of voices singing in rounds. The bogans kept up a "dum-dum-dum" rhythm that the prisoners were forced to march to. From what conversation they could make out amidst all the noise, they learned that while Eilian was bound for the Big Men's amusement, and Jacky as well, the rest of them were to meet another fate.

> A slice of an ear and a shaving of spleen,
>   smell that stew, oh smell it now;
> now chop up the entrails, just a tad, it never fails
>   —better than sheep, ho! Better than a cow!

> Sucking on a marrow bone while it cooks,
>   smell that stew, oh smell it now!

The tunnel opened up into a well-lit area—a gigantic cavern that reeked like a raw sewer and was filled with capering creatures, grinning bogans, hungry-eyed hags, and other monsters they hadn't seen yet that day. Goblins and knockers, trolls and black-bearded duergar, all yammering and pushing forward to see the captives.

"BACK OFF! BACK OFF!" Thundell roared, swiping the creatures out of the way with wide blows of his big hands.

A space cleared around them. Breathing through her mouth, Kate lifted her head wearily. Every bone and muscle in her body ached from bruises. The place was a nightmare of sight and smell and sound. And there, sitting at the far end of the cavern on a throne cut directly from its rock wall, was the largest and ugliest of the monsters yet.

She didn't need anyone to tell her who this was: Gyre the Elder, greasy-haired, with a nose almost as big as the rest of his face. A hunch back that rose up behind his head. Hands, each the size of a kitchen tabletop. Chin and nose festooned with warts, some almost four inches long. If she had been at home and run across this creature in a picture book, she would have laughed. As it was, her legs gave way and she fell to her knees on the hard rock ground.

The two giants conversed, but it was like listening to thunder roaring in the confines of the cavern and she never did hear what it was they said. They could have been speaking Swahili for all she knew. She would have fallen full length on the ground, but a bogan snared his thick fingers in her short hair and pulled her head upright. The whole weight of her body hung from his hand. Then just as she was getting used to the thunder, to the pain, she was hauled to her feet and they were led forward.

Dragged in front of Gyre the Elder, Kate stared blearily at him, unable to keep her eyes from his ugliness. The worst thing about him—the absolute worst—was that his eyes were totally mad. But clever-looking too. Sly, like a weasel's, or a rat's.

Numbly, just as she was shoved past him and out of his sight, she saw the small ivory of a horn hanging on the wall behind him. She blinked as she looked at it, knowing it meant something, but no longer able to remember exactly what it was. It appeared to be discoloured with red dots, as though someone had splattered blood over it and not bothered to clean it. Then the bogan behind her gave her a shove that drove her into Arkan's back and the horn was gone, out of her view. She forgot it as she fought to stay on her feet.

They were pushed and prodded down a narrower corridor, then finally herded into a chamber cut out of the rock wall that had a great wooden grating for a door. The bogans threw them into the room where they fell on the damp straw strewn across the floor. The wooden grating closed with a jarring crash. A great beam of wood that took five bogans to lift was set into place, barring the door, and then finally they were alone. Blessedly alone.

It was a long time before Kate even had the energy, little say the inclination, to sit up. Then it was something snuffling in the straw near her that made her push herself rapidly away from the source of the sound, her rear end scraping the floor while she pushed with her feet.

"Moon and stars!" Arkan cried. "What is it?"

Creeping forward was a piglike creature. It was a dirty white, eyes rimmed with red and wild looking—mad eyes, not like Gyre the Elder's which were sly as well, but mad eyes of a hurt and broken creature from whom most sense had fled. It was trussed with a nettle coat like Eilian's. Belly on the ground, the creature moved slowly towards them, snuffling and moaning.

"No!" Kate shrieked as it came closer to her.

The thing backed away making whimpering noises that sounded all too human for comfort.

Beside Kate, Eilian gazed at it, horrified. "I . . . I think we've found the Laird of Kinrowan's daughter," he said.

"Th-that? But it . . . it's a pig."

"And once it had Laird's blood—why else bind it with a nettle coat?"

Bile rose in Kate's throat as she looked at the pitiable thing. "Why . . . why isn't it part swan, then?" she asked. "Like you?"

"Because they've changed her," Arkan said. "Their Gruagagh's changed her."

He moved closer to Kate as he spoke. Grunting with the effort, he tried to bring his bound hands around in front of him, but his hips were too wide for the maneuver. He backed up to her then, and began to work at the leather binding her hands.

"That wasn't a Huntsman that caught Jacky," he said as he fumbled at the knots with numbed fingers.

"How can you be sure?" Kate asked.

She couldn't take her gaze from the piggish thing that might once have been Lorana if the others were to be believed. It was emaciated, reminding her of the pictures she'd seen of starving people in Africa or India.

"That's what the giants were arguing about before they had us put in here," Arkan replied. "We've been spared for the moment because the whole Court's going out to hunt her down."

Suddenly Kate's hands were free. She brought them around in front of her, rubbing the chaffed wrists. Prickles of pain started up in her hands as her circulation returned.

"Why don't they use the Hunt?" she asked.

"They're missing a rider. Whoever took Jacky away had one of their motorcycles. Moon knows what her captor did with the rider. If he managed to kill it—which is very unlikely—she'll be safe from the Hunt. For awhile, at least. When one of their number's slain . . . They don't work as well unless all nine are alive and gathered."

It was taking Kate a lot longer to remove Arkan's bonds than it had taken him to undo hers. She kept staring at every noise she heard. My nerves are shot, she thought. Finished. Kaput. And whenever the piggish thing snuffled, she could feel her skin crawling. But at last she had Arkan free. Then she removed the nettle coat from Eilian while Arkan untied Finn.

"I know it'd come to no good, talking to that girl," Finn muttered as he was freed. "All her talk about rescuing this and doing that, and here we all are, trapped in the Big Men's own Keep—damn their stone hearts—and where's she? Running free, is where. And far from here if she has any sense."

"That's unfair to say," Eilian said before Kate could voice her own sharper retort to the hob. "She led us, yes, but we followed of our own will. And it wasn't part of her plan to get snatched away while we were all ambushed."

"She had no plan," Finn said. "And that's where all the trouble began. Just pushing in here and pushing in there— oh, I admire her pluck, yes, I do—but there was never a hope. Just look at us now—ready for the stewpots if those gully-wudes have us, worse I'm sure, if the Big Men decide they want us. And our Jack herself, out being hunted up dale and down by everything from Big Men to the Wild Hunt itself, I don't doubt. Oh, it's a bad time we're in the middle of, and the end'll only be worse.''

Arkan had been investigating the grated wooden door while Finn was complaining. He turned back and shook his head at Eilian's unspoken question. "There's no way out through that—not unless we can match the strength of five bogans.''

"I won't go easy this time," Eilian said. "They'll not do to me what they did to this poor soul. I'll hang myself first.''

All gazes turned to their cellmate. The ugly head of the creature scraped the ground as it backed fearfully away from them, belly to the ground. Kate took a deep breath, let it out. She swallowed, then moved slowly forward.

"There, there," she said to it. Someone had to do something for it. "We won't hurt you. How could we, you poor thing? Come here. Don't be afraid of me. Kate won't hurt you.''

It trembled as she approached, but no longer tried to back away. Forcing her stomach to keep down what wanted to come up her gorge, Kate reached for the creature, stroked the rough skin of its head as she worked at undoing its nettle coat. Her hands were already stinging from removing Eilian's and now the pain was worse—sharp, like hundreds of little knives piercing her skin.

She wasn't afraid of the creature anymore—not as she had been at first. And even her repugnance faded, now that she could feel it tremble under her hands. It wasn't its fault that it was in this predicament—any more than it was their own. But oh, what would the Gruagagh do if this was all that had become of his Laird's daughter? Samhaine Eve was just a couple of weeks away, and the lot of them all trapped anyway. Except for Jacky. And though Jacky had killed a giant and been lucky in everything so far, what could she really do against the hordes of the Unseelie Court that were out there looking for her now?

The last fastening came loose and she tugged the coat from the creature. Its shape began to change, the emaciated pig's body becoming a sickly-thin woman's. But the head—the head didn't change at all.

"Are there beings like this in either of the faerie Courts?" Kate asked her companions as she held the trembling woman with the pig's head against her shoulder. The creature burrowed its face in the folds of Kate's torn clothing.

Eilian shook his head. "She's been enchanted—evilly enchanted."

"By a gruagagh?" Kate asked.

"Or a witch."

Kate put her head close to the woman's. "Can you speak?" she asked. "Who did this to you? Who are you? Please don't be afraid. We won't hurt you."

"Ugly." The one word came out, muffled and low.

Kate forced a smile into her voice. "You think you're ugly? Haven't you seen that monstrosity lording it over his Court out there? Now that's ugly! Not you."

There was a long pause before the muffled voice said, "I saw . . . your face. I saw my ugliness reflected in your eyes."

Kate stroked the dry pig skin of the woman's head. "I was scared then—that's all." She looked over at Arkan. "Give us your jacket, would you? The poor thing's got nothing on—no wonder she's scared. Bunch of jocks like you gawking at her." Arkan passed her his jacket and she wrapped it around her charge. "We want to help you," she said. "We're all in here together, you know, so we might as well try to get along. My name's Kate Hazel. What's yours?"

The pig's head lifted to look Kate in the eye. Kate steeled her features and refused to let any repugnance show. In fact, it wasn't so hard. She felt so bad for the poor woman that she didn't see her as ugly anymore, for all that it *was* still a pig's head. She schooled herself not to show pity either. Strangely enough, feeling protective for this poor creature, she'd ended up losing her own fears about being trapped here in the Giants' Keep.

"Make up a name," she said, "if you don't want to tell us your real one. Just so we can call you something."

The creature swallowed nervously. Its gaze darted to the others in the cell, then back to Kate.

"I . . . I'm Gyre the Elder's daughter," she said finally.

CHAPTER
18

Clinging to the back of what might be either her benefactor or captor, with the rough texture of his twig and leaf coat stickily against her and the wind rushing by her ears with a gale-like force, all Jacky could do was hold on for dear life. They were going too fast for her to dare jumping off. But as the ambush fell further and further behind them and, with it, her captured, maybe hurt—please, God, not dead—friends, her fear for her own safety got buried under a wave of anger. When the Harley began to slow down about a half-mile past the gravel pit, she dared to let go of a hand and whacked the stranger on the back.

"Let me go!" she shouted in his ear.

The motorcycle came to a skidding halt along the side of the road, so abruptly that they almost both toppled off. Jacky hopped from her seat and ran a few steps away from the machine. She wanted to take off, but after what had happened back at the bridge, and with this new as yet undefined being facing her, she wasn't quite sure what she should do. The stranger, for his part, merely smiled, and pushed the Harley into the ditch. Jacky swallowed nervously when she spotted his cloven feet.

"Who—who are you?" she asked.

"I have a pocket full of names," he replied, grinning.

Like most of the faerie Jacky had met so far, there was

something indefinable in his eyes, something that she was never sure she could trust.

"I wonder which you'd like to hear?" the stranger added, thrusting one hand into a deep pocket. "A Jackish one won't do—you having a Jackish name yourself—but perhaps Tom Coof?"

He pulled something from his pocket and tossed it into the air too quickly for Jacky to see what it was. A fine dust sprinkled down, covering him, and then he appeared like a village simpleton to her.

"Or maybe Cappy Rag would please you better?" he asked. "A bit of a Gypsy, you know, but more kindly than some I could be."

Again the hand went into the pocket, out again and up into the air. When the new dust settled, he was wearing a wild coat that was covered with multi-coloured, many-lengthed ribbons, all tattery and bright. He did a quick spin, ribbons flying in a whirl of colour, dizzying Jacky.

"Or perhaps—"

But Jacky cut him off. When he'd done his little spin, she'd seen the bag hanging from his shoulder, recognized the shape of the thing it held.

"Or perhaps your name is Kerevan," she said, "and you play the fiddle as well as the fool. What do you want with me?"

Kerevan shrugged, showing no surprise that she knew his name. The ribbon coat became a coat of heather, twigs and leaves.

"I made a bargain," he said. "To see you to the Giants' Keep."

"A bargain? With whom? And what about my friends?"

"The bargain didn't include anyone else."

"And who did you make this bargain with?"

"Can't say."

Bhruic, perhaps? Jacky thought. Only why he would do this, why he'd disappeared from the Tower . . . none of this made sense. And what if it hadn't been Bhruic? It was so hard to think. But she was sure of one thing: She didn't want anything to do with this—she glanced at the hooves again—whatever he was. She looked back down the road they'd travelled, but they'd gone too far for her to see what had become of her friends and the attacking Host. Then, before Kerevan could stop her, she slipped on her hob-stitched coat and disappeared from sight.

"Then think about this," her bodiless voice called out to him, "You didn't see me to the Giants' Keep and I'm not going with you, so your side of this bargain will never be completed."

Hob-stitched shoes helped her slip swiftly up the pavement from where she'd been standing.

"You can't do this!" Kerevan cried. "You mustn't!"

He tossed a powder towards where she'd been standing, but it fluttered uselessly to the ground, revealing nothing because she wasn't there.

"Who did you bargain with?" Jacky called, moving with magical quickness as she spoke. "And what was the bargain?"

By the time Kerevan reached the spot she'd been, she was away down the road again. She looked back, expecting him to at least be trying to pursue her, but instead he took his fiddle from its bag, then the bow. He tightened the hairs of the bow, but before he could draw it across the strings, Jacky had her fingers in her ears. She could hear what he was playing, not loudly, but audible all the same.

There was a spell in the music. It said, *Take off your coat. Lie down and sleep. What a weary day it's been. That coat will make a fine pillow, now won't it just?*

If she hadn't had her fingers in her ears, the spell would have worked. But she'd been prepared, cutting down the potency of the spell by cutting down the volume, as well as being mentally prepared for, if not exactly this, well then, at least something.

She moved silently closer, soft-stepping like a cat, watching the growing consternation on the fiddler's face. She was close to him now. Very close. Taking a deep breath, she reached forward suddenly, snatching the fiddle from his grasp, and took off again, with a hob's stealth and speed.

"This is a stupid game!" she called to him, changing position after every few words. "Why don't you go home and leave me alone? Go back and tell Bhruic that I *am* going to the Giants' Keep and I don't need fools like you getting in the way. And I don't need him, either."

"But—"

"Go on, or I'll break this thing."

"Please, oh, please don't!"

"Why shouldn't I? You've stolen me away from my friends—they could be captured or dead or God knows what and all you do is stand around playing stupid word games when I ask you a civil question. Thank you for helping me escape. Now get out of my life or I'll smash this fiddle of yours—I swear I will!"

Kerevan sat down on the side of the road. He laid his bow on the gravel in front of him and emptied his pockets. What grew in a pile beside the bow looked like a heap of pebbles, but they were all soft and a hundred different colours. There was magic in them, in each one, Jacky knew. She moved closer, still silent.

"A bargain," Kerevan said. "My fiddle for the answers to whatever you want." When there was no reply, he pointed to the pile. "These are wally-stanes," he said. "Not quartz or stone, and not playthings, but magics—my magics. They're filled with dusts that can catch an invisible Jack or change a shape, or even a name. They're yours—just give me the fiddle and let me see you safe to the Giants' Keep."

"Why?"

"Why, why, why! What does it matter why? The bargain's a good one. The fiddle's no use to you, without the kenning, and I doubt you know the kenning, now do you? But these wally-stanes any fool can use, even a Jack, and there's a power in them, power you'll need before the night's through."

Again there was a silence. Then Jacky spoke once more, this time from a dozen feet away from where her voice had come when it had asked why.

"This is the bargain I'll offer," she said. "Your fiddle, for my safety from you, for the wally-stanes, and for the knowledge of who you had your first bargain with—the bargain to see me safely to the keep," she amended quickly.

Kerevan's smile faded as she caught herself. His first bargain would have been easy. That was his bargain with life and with it he'd gotten born. Oh, this was no fool, this Jack, or the right kind of fool, depending on how you juggled your tricks.

"That's too much for an old fiddle," he said.

"Well, I'll just be going then," Jacky replied.

She was standing almost directly behind now and startled him with her proximity. Kerevan wanted—oh, very badly—to turn around and try to nab her, but he thought better of it. She was no fool, and she was quick too. But he remembered now, while he'd been looking for her, with more senses than just his eyes, he had sensed something he thought he could use.

"Let me show you a thing," he said. "Let me take you to a place nearby and show you something—no tricks now, and this is a promise from one puck to another."

How can I trust you? Jacky wanted to ask, but she was standing in front of him at the time, looking into his eyes, and knew—without knowing how, while thinking, oh, you're a fool, indeed, and not the kind Kerevan meant either—that she had to trust him. Yet she'd trusted the Gruagagh . . .

"All right," she said finally. "But I'm keeping the fiddle."

"Fair enough." He tossed the bag out towards her voice. "But store it in this, would you? There's a fair bit of my heart in that wee instrument and if you chip it or bang it, you'll be chipping away bits of me."

Jacky caught the cloth and stuffed the fiddle into it. Then before she slung it over her shoulder, she removed her blue jacket and stood in front of him on the road.

"What's this thing we're going to see?" she asked, worried that she was making a big mistake.

"It's a seeing one, not a talking one," Kerevan replied. "Come follow me."

He scooped up his wally-stanes and replaced them in his pockets, snatched up his bow, then took off into the woods at a brisk pace that Jacky, if she hadn't had her hob-stitched sneakers on, would have been hard-pressed to follow. They darted in and out between the trees, the ground growing steadily steeper as they went.

"Quiet now," Kerevan whispered, coming to a sudden halt.

Jacky bumped into him. "What is it?"

"We're close now—to bogans and gullywudes and all the other stone-hearted bastards that make up the Unseelie Court."

He crept ahead then, moving so quietly that, if Jacky hadn't known he was there, she would never have noticed him. And she, city kid though she was, found herself keeping up with him, as quiet, as slyly, as secret, with no great effort on her part. Hobbery magics, she told herself. Cap and shoes and jacket on my arm. But a voice inside her murmured, once perhaps, but no longer just that.

This time when Kerevan stopped, Jacky was ready for it. She crept up beside him, and peered through the brush to see what he was looking at. One fleeting glance was all she took before she quickly looked away. She wanted to throw up.

There was a clearing ahead, an opening in the trees where a cliff face was bared to the sky. There were bogans there, and a giant snoring against a tree, and other creatures besides, but it wasn't they who disturbed her. It was what was on the cliff face itself.

Once she might have been beautiful—perhaps she still was under the dirt and dried blood. But now, hung like an offering—like Balder from his tree, like Christ from his cross, like all those bright things sacrificed to the darkness—a swan-armed woman was bound to wooden stakes driven into the stone. She hung a half-dozen feet from the ground, her clothes in ragged tatters, but the nettle tunic, oh, it was new and tightly bound around her torso. The swan wings were a soiled white, as was the hair that hung in dirty strands to either side of her emaciated face. The flesh of her legs was broken with cuts and sores. Her face was bruised and cut as well. And she was—this was the worst—she was still alive. Hanging there, on the stone wall of a cliff that was stained with white bird droppings, many of which had splattered on her, surrounded by the jeering Unseelie Court that had had its pleasure mocking and hurting her for so long that they were tired of the sport.

She was still alive.

Acid roiled in Jacky's stomach. Tremours shook her. In another moment she might have screamed from the sheer horror of that sight, but Kerevan touched her shoulder, soothed her with the faintest hum of a tune that he lipped directly against her ear, then soundlessly led her back, away, higher, into the wilderness. She leaned against him for a long while before she could walk on her own again, and then they

still moved on, travelling through progressively wilder country until they came to a gorge that cut like a blade through
the mountainous slopes.

It was heavily treed with birch and cedar and pine, and
Kerevan led her into it. The fiddler sat her down on some
grass by a stone that she could lean against. He came back
with water cupped in his hands, made her drink, went for
more, returned. Three times he made her drink. At any time
he could have retrieved his bagged fiddle and been gone, but
there were bargains to uphold, and now a shared horror that
bound them, not to each other, but to something that was
almost the same.

"My bargain," Kerevan said suddenly, "is with the Gruagagh of Kinrowan. Did you know he meant to be a poet
before he took on the cloak of spells he wears now? No other
would wear it and it had to be one of Kinrowan blood, so he
took it. He kept Kinrowan alive, shared the ceremonies with
Lorana. Between the two of them they kept a light shining in
the dark.

"But the time for light is gone, Jacky Rowan. That was
Lorana we saw there, and that will be Bhruic too. That will
be the Laird of Kinrowan, that will be every being with
Lairdsblood, and probably that will be Jacky Rowan too.
There is no stopping it."

Jacky couldn't drive the terrible vision from her. "But if
we freed her . . ."

"That would only prolong what will be. The time of darkness has come to our world -to Faerie. They moved here
from the crowded moors and highlands of their old homeland
when the mortals came to this open land. But the Host followed too and here, here the Unseelie Court grows stronger
than ever before. Would you know why? Because your kind
will always believe in evil before it believes in good. There
are so many of you in this land, so many feeding the darkness
. . . the time for the Seelie Court can almost be measured in
days now."

"I don't understand," Jacky said. "I know what you
mean about the evil feeding on belief, but if Lorana was
freed . . ."

"They have the Horn. They rule the Wild Hunt. Nothing
can withstand the Hunt. For a while a power like Bhruic

wields could, or my fiddle might, but when they are set upon the trail of some being, mortal or faerie, that being is dead. They *never* fail.''

"So we have to steal the Horn."

"Listening to Bhruic, I thought so once, Jacky Rowan. But the Horn is too great a power. It corrupts any being who wields it. It corrupts any being who even holds it for safe-keeping.''

"But Bhruic . . ."

"Wanted the Horn to find Lorana. She was his charge; he was responsible for her.''

Jacky frowned. "And you've known where she was all the time and said nothing to him. How could you? She's been suffering for months! Jesus Christ, what kind of a thing are you?''

"I don't know what I am, Jacky Rowan, but I never knew she was there until we stood on the road, you and I, and I strained all my senses to find you. Instead I caught a glimmer that was her. They hide her well, with glamours and bind-ings.''

"But now we know," Jacky said. "Now we can help her.''

"You and I? Are we an army then?''

"What about your fiddle? And your wally-stanes?''

"They're tricks—nothing more. Mending magics, making magics—not greatspells used for war.''

Jacky stared away into the trees, seeing the tormented face of the Laird of Kinrowan's daughter no matter where she looked, and knew that she'd do anything to help her.

"If I had the Horn," she asked, "could I use it to com-mand the Hunt to free her?''

"You could. And then what would you command? That all the Unseelie Court be slain? That any who disagree with you be slain? You may call me a coward, Jacky Rowan, but I wouldn't touch that Horn for any bargain. Use it once and it will burn your soul forevermore.''

"Bargain . . ." She looked at him then. "Tell me about your bargain with Bhruic.''

"In exchange for what?''

"Tell me!''

Kerevan regarded her steadily. The fierceness in her gaze gave him true pause. Here was gruagagh material . . . or another wasted poet turned to war. But that was always the way with Jacks, wasn't it? They were clever and fools all at once. But the image of Lorana's torment had stayed with him as well, and so he made no bargains, only replied.

"I was to bring you safe to the Keep and then he was to come with me."

"Where to?"

"To where I am when I'm not here—that's not a question I'll answer, nor even bargain to answer for, Jacky Rowan, so save your breath."

She nodded. "This is my bargain then: I'll return your fiddle, for safety from you and for some of your wally-stanes."

"That's all?"

"That's all."

"And you'll let me lead you to the Keep?"

"I have to go to the Keep. My friends are there, if they're still alive. And the Horn's there."

"Girl, you don't know what you're talking about. That Horn is no toy."

"*Boy*, you'll take the bargain my way, or your fiddle will lie in pieces from here to wherever the hell it was that you came from in the first place."

They glared at each other, neither giving an inch, then suddenly Kerevan nodded.

"Done!" he said. "What care I what you do in that Keep or with that Horn? I want the Lairdlings to be safe--all of Lairdsblood—and whoever will come with me, by their own desire or if I must trick them, those will be saved. But not by doing what you do. Not by the Horn."

"Running away from what you have to face doesn't solve anything."

"And running headlong into it does? Willy-nilly, and mad is as mad does? Oh, I wish you well, Jacky Rowan, but I doubt we'll meet again in this world."

"I don't know," Jacky said. "You seem to do pretty good moving from one to the other."

"What do you mean by that?"

"I was told you'd died about a hundred and fifty years ago, but I get the feeling that, even if you *did* die back then, with you it's never permanent."

"I'm no god—"

"I know. You're Tom Coof and Cappy Rag and you're full of tricks and bargains. I think you might even mean well in what you do, Kerevan, but sometimes I think you're too damn clever for your own good—you know what I mean?"

Before he could answer, she stood up and offered him his fiddle. "Come on," she added. "I want to get inside the Keep before it gets dark."

"There'll be an uproar," Kerevan said. "They'll be scouring the countryside, looking for you."

"Well, then. If you want to keep your bargain with Bhruic, you'd better start thinking about how you're going to get me in there in one piece, don't you think?"

Kerevan considered himself a manipulator, one who cajoled, or tricked, or somehow got everyone to follow a pattern that he had laid out and only he could see. It was worse than disconcerting to have his own tricks played back on himself. He took his fiddle bag, returned his bow to it, and slung it over his shoulder. Taking out his wally-stanes, he let her choose as many as she wanted. She took nine.

Three times three, he thought. She knows too much, or something else is moving through her, but either way he was caught with his own bargains and could only follow through the pattern that was unwinding before him now.

"Come along, then," he said, and he led her back into the forest once more.

CHAPTER
19

"His daughter?" Arkan said, staring at the pig-headed woman. "Oh, that's just bloody grand, isn't it?"

"Arkan, be still," Eilian said softly.

Kate, looking from the poor creature to the two faerie, was suddenly struck by what a difference Lairdsblood made. Arkan, brash and not easily cowed except by the Gruagagh, had immediately obeyed Eilian's quiet statement. She could see the distaste blooming in his eyes, but he said not another word as Eilian came to where she sat with the giant's daughter.

"If they're not born Big Men, and strong," Eilian said, "oh, it's a hard lot to be a giant's child."

The creature tried to hide her features in the crook of Kate's shoulder as he leaned closer, but he cupped her chin and made her look at him.

"You weren't born this way," he said. "Who set the shape-spell on you?"

"The Gruagagh," she said.

Kate gasped. "The Gruagagh?" Her worst fears were realized. Bhruic Dearg *had* set them up.

"I warned you," Finn muttered. "But would anyone listen?"

"Not so quickly," Eilian said. "There is more than one gruagagh, just as there's more than one Billy Blind. It's like

157

saying weaver or carpenter—no more.'' He turned back to
the creature. "Which gruagagh? One in your father's Court?''

The creature nodded.

"That could still be Bhruic Dearg,'' Arkan said. "For all
we know he—'' He broke off as Eilian shot him a hard look.

"And what's your name?'' the Laird's son asked the creature, gentling his features as he looked at her once more.

"Monster,'' she said gruffly and tried to look away, but
Eilian wouldn't let her.

"We came here to help another,'' he said, "but we won't
leave you like this when we go. We'll help you, too.''

"And how will we do that, Laird's son?'' Arkan asked,
emboldened by the fact that there was no way Eilian could
make good such a promise. "Even if we had spells, you
know as well as I that Seelie magic'll never take hold in this
place. We can't help her. We can't even help ourselves.''

"Be still!'' Eilian cried, his eyes flashing with anger. "We
have a Jack with us,'' he said to the giant's daughter, "loose
outside the Keep and she'll help us. Don't listen to him.''

"A Jack,'' Finn repeated mournfully. "And what can she
do, Eilian? Didn't you see the Court Gyre's gathered here?
All it needs is sluagh to make its evil complete—and they'll
be here come nightfall.''

"Our Jack's all we have,'' Eilian repeated quietly. "Let's
at least lend the strength of our belief to her, if nothing else.
What's your name?'' he tried again, returning his attention
to the giant's ensorceled daughter.

There was no escaping the Lairdling's gaze. It penetrated
the creature's fears, burning them away.

"Moddy Gill,'' she said.

"That's a nice name,'' Kate offered for lack of anything
better to say. The creature gave her a grateful look.

"And a powerful one, too,'' Eilian added. "There was a
Moddy Gill that once withstood the Samhaine dead, all alone
and that whole night—do you know the tale?'' Moddy Gill
shook her head. "It was a bargain she made with the Laird
of Fincastle. One night alone against the Samhaine dead and
if she survived, she could have what she wanted from the
Laird, be it his own child.''

"What . . . what did she take?'' Moddy Gill asked.

"His black dog,'' Eilian replied with a grin. "And with it

at her side, she stormed Caern Rue and won free the prince-ling from the Kinnair Trow. Oh, it's a good story and one I never tired of hearing from our Billy Blind. They married, those two, and went into the west with the black dog. No one knows what befell them there, but do you know what I think?''

Moddy Gill shook her head. She was sitting upright now, just leaning a bit against Kate.

"I think that if they didn't live happily ever after, they at least lived happily, and for a very long time. And so will you, Moddy Gill. We'll take you with us when we leave this Keep.''

"You came for the swangirl, didn't you?'' she asked.

"In part,'' Eilian replied. "But we came to make an end of the Unseelie Court here as well.''

"Is she your girl?'' Moddy Gill asked.

"Who? Lorana?'' Eilian laughed. "I doubt she knows I exist. I came here to help our dear Jack, not looking for swangirls to wed.''

Kate gave him a considering look. There was something in his voice when he spoke of Jacky that made her think that he had more in mind than simply helping her.

"I know something,'' Moddy Gill said. Her pig's head was nodding thoughtfully, the tiny eyes fixing their gaze on Eilian. "I know where they keep the Laird of Kinrowan's daughter. They hang her out by day, but not at night. Then they put her in a cell—a secret cell—and I know where it is.''

"When our Jack comes, will you help us rescue her?''

Moddy Gill sighed. The sound was a long wheezing snuf-fle. "We'll never get free,'' she said. "And the night's com-ing soon when they'll give her to the Samhaine dead and then they'll stew *us* for their feast.''

"Well, at least someone's speaking sense here,'' Arkan said.

Kate frowned at him. "Why are you being like this?'' she demanded. "I thought you were going to help.''

"And I wanted to help, make no mistake about it, Kate. Your courage made me feel small, but moon and stars! I remember now why I had such a lack of it myself. We were helpless against the horde that ambushed us, and they were but a drop in the bucket compared to the size of the Court Gyre has gathered in this place.''

"We've no magics here," Finn explained. "Not hob magics, nor Laird's magics—nothing saintly. Not even a gruagagh's spells will take hold in a place so fouled by the Host.''

"Then we'll just have to depend on something other than magic," Kate said.

Eilian nodded grimly. "Until we're dead, there's hope.''

Arkan looked as though he meant to continue the argument, but then he shrugged. "Why not?" he said. "I heard a poet say once that we make our own fortunes and if our future goes bleak, we've ourselves to blame as much as anything else. 'Be true to your beliefs,' he said, 'and you'll win through.' They're just words, I thought then, and I think so now, but sometimes words have power—when they fall from the proper lips. I'll mourn our deaths no more—not until the blade falls on my neck.''

"Oh, they won't use axes," Moddy Gill said. "They like to throw folks in their stews while they're still kicking—for the flavour, you know.''

"And have you tasted such a stew?" Eilian asked.

Moddy Gill shook her head. "I've no taste for another's pain, Lairdling. Not when knowing so much of my own.''

Kate patted the girl's shoulder, then stood up to investigate the wooden grating that served for the door to their prison. The beams were as thick as a large man's thighs, notched together, then bound in place by heavy ropes that appeared to be woven from leather thonging rather than twine. The beam that lay across the door, held by a stone slot at either end, had taken five bogans to set in place. They didn't have close to that kind of brute strength in their own small company.

"Why did they just use rope?" she asked Eilian as he joined her.

"Faerie can't abide iron.''

"And even steel's got a high iron count—big enough to make no difference," Kate said with a considering nod. She turned to Eilian. "But what about those bridges the trolls live under—and the buildings in the cities? There's iron in all of them.''

"True enough. Faerie that live in or near your cities and

towns come to acquire a resistance to it. Some can simply abide a proximity to it, but can't handle it themselves. Others, like our forester here, seem to have developed a total immunity—how else could he use your vehicle with such ease?''

Her car. Judith was dead and gone now. ''And what about the Host?'' she asked.

''They're a wilder faerie, not always used to urban ways. Against many, a penknife would be enough defense.''

There was a long moment's silence, then Kate grinned and reached into her pocket. ''Like this?'' she asked.

She opened her hand to show her Swiss penknife. Opened, it had a blade length of two inches. She could have kicked herself for not thinking of it earlier when they were struggling with their bonds. But it didn't matter. They had it now.

''Oh, Kate!'' Eilian replied. His eyes shone with delight. ''Exactly like that.''

''But these ropes are so thick . . .''

''They were woven with faerie magic. Even your little blade there will have no trouble cutting through them.''

''All *right*.''

She pried the blade out of its handle and began to saw away at the nearest rope. The others gathered round to watch the little knife cut through the first thick cord as though it were no more than a piece of string. Moddy Gill regarded Kate with awe.

''Moon and stars!'' Arkan said. ''When I find that poet, I'll gift him with enough ale to keep him drunk for a fortnight.''

Finn nodded eagerly. ''This hope's a potent magic all on its own,'' he said.

Arkan grinned. ''And the next time you hear me whispering against it, Kate, just give me a good strong clout across the back of my head.''

''With pleasure,'' Kate said as she continued to saw away at the ropes.

She didn't bother to mention that once they got out of their cell their troubles would be just beginning. There was no point in dashing their sudden enthusiasm. But they were going to have to come up with something more than a little Swiss penknife before they got out of this place. And then there was Jacky. Had the bogans caught her as well? Or was that strange being that had snatched her on the highway one of the Wild Hunt in another guise? She had the sinking feeling that the nightmare was just starting to get under way.

CHAPTER
20

"What's up now, Tom Coof?" Jacky asked in a whisper.

"Whisht—just for once," the fiddler hissed back at her.

They were hidden in undergrowth, high up in the forest and rough terrain that was, Jacky supposed, near the Giants' Keep. The land was certainly wild enough. The tree covering was mostly pine and cedar, with some hardwoods. Granite outcrops jutted from the ground like the elbows of buried stone giants. Roots twisted around the outcrops; deadfalls surrounded them. It had taken them the better part of the afternoon to get here from the road—Jacky in her hob jacket and Kerevan using his own spells. The forest was alive with the creatures of the Host, searching for her.

Jacky was just about to repeat her question when she saw what had driven them into hiding once more. As tall as some of the trees around them, a giant came, moving with deceptive quiet for all his huge bulk. He sniffed the air, a nose the size of Jacky's torso quivering. Jacky stopped breathing. Finally the giant moved on. Gullywudes and bogans moved in his wake. Not until they were five minutes gone did Kerevan speak.

"Do you see that small gap? There—just the other side of the deadfall?" he whispered.

"In the rocks there?"

Kerevan nodded, but neither of them could see each other, so the motion was wasted. "That's one of their bolt holes," he said. "Take it and follow it into the heart of the mountain and it will bring you straight to where Gyre the Elder holds his Court."

Jacky bit at her lower lip, which was getting all too much wear of late. "You're leaving me here?"

"This is the Giants' Keep. You *did* want to come here, remember?"

"Yes, but . . ." She sighed. Somehow she'd hoped that, once they'd reached the place, Kerevan would change his mind and offer to help her.

"A word of warning," the fiddler added. "Seelie magics are of no use inside—so your hob coat won't hide you, your shoes won't speed you, your cap won't show you any new secrets, and even the wally-stanes you took from me will do you no good. Not when you're inside."

"Is that why you won't go in?"

"It's suicide to go in there," he replied. "A fool I might be, but I'm not mad."

Jacky looked in his direction. If she squinted and looked very hard she could just make out the vague outline of his shape.

"I don't know what to do," she said. "Now that I'm here, I don't know what to do, or where to begin. Can't you give me some advice—or does that require another bargain?"

"This advice is free: Go home and forget this place."

"I can't."

"Then do what you must do, Jacky Rowan, and pray you didn't use up all your luck these past few days."

"And nothing will work—I mean, none of the magics?"

"Not one." Kerevan sighed. "There was a reason that no Seelie's gone to do what you mean to try, and now you know it. It's not so much a lack of courage—though the Seelies left are not so brave as once their folk were, and who can blame them? Once in that Keep, they would be powerless. You've seen the Big Men. You've seen their Court—the bogans and all. How could hobs and brownies and the like stand up against them, without their spells to help them? Even Bhruic would have no more than his natural strength in there."

"Okay, okay. You've made your point. I go by myself and it's kamikaze time."

Kerevan knew what she meant, that it was a suicide mission, but he said: "Do you know the actual meaning of that word? 'Divine Wind.' Perhaps you should call on the gods to help you."

"I don't believe in God. At least I don't think I do," she added, hedging.

"The desert god your people hung from a tree couldn't help you here anyway," Kerevan replied. "This is the land of the Manitou. But Mabon walks that Great Mystery's woods sometimes and the Moon is sacred everywhere."

"Is Mabon your god?"

"Mabon is the young horned lord."

Jacky gave him a quizzical look, but he didn't elaborate. "I guess that when I go down that hole," she said, "it's just going to be me and no one else."

"I fear you're right."

"Then I suppose it's time I got my ass in gear and got to it."

An invisible hand touched her shoulder and gave it a squeeze. "Go lucky as your name can take you," Kerevan said.

Jacky swallowed. "Thanks for getting me here," she said. "I know you were just fulfilling your bargain with Bhruic, but thanks all the same."

"I mean you no ill, Jacky Rowan, and I never have."

There was nothing more to say, so she moved ahead, past the deadfall to the gap in the rocks. There was a passage of some sort there. A familiar reck rose out of it. This has got to be the way, she thought, because nothing else could smell this bad. Breathing through her mouth, she squeezed between the rocks and forced her way in. The passage wasn't high enough to stand in, so she moved forward at a crouch, one hand on the wall to her left, the other brushing the ground ahead of her.

Kerevan sighed when she was gone. He touched his fiddle, felt the stag's head scroll through the cloth material of its bag. He was free to go now. He had done all that he'd bargained to do. Yet he stayed hidden in the underbrush, staring at the bolt-hole. After a long while, he sighed again, then began moving slowly up along the rocky mountainside, head-

ing for the great stone gates that were the main entrance to
the Keep.

There's fools and there's fools, he told himself as he went.
And here I am, all these years old, and I never knew I was
still *this* sort of a fool.

The smell intensified, the deeper Jacky went down the narrow tunnel. If this was a bolthole, she thought, it could only
be one for little creatures, because a bogan wouldn't fit in
and a giant would have trouble just sticking his arm into it.
She'd never been one of those people that got nervous in an
enclosed space, but this tunnel, with the weight of a mountain
on top of it, had her shivering. Combined with the darkness
and the stench, and with what she knew lay waiting for her
at the tunnel's end, there were half a dozen times when she
thought she would take Kerevan's advice after all. She was
ready to just GoJackyGo right out of here.

But then she remembered the pitiful figure of Lorana,
hanging from the cliff. Not to mention the fact that Kate and
the rest were probably trapped down here somewhere. Not to
mention that the Host was out to get her personally now. Not
to mention . . . oh, it made her head ache just to think of it
all.

Her watch didn't have a luminous dial so she couldn't even
tell what time it was, or how long she'd been down this hole.
It seemed like forever. It had been getting dark when she first
crawled in—that time when shadows grow long but it's still
not quite twilight yet. It could be midnight now, for all she
knew. But the stench kept getting stronger, so she knew she
was getting somewhere. And she'd begun to hear a noise—a
booming sort of sound that rose and fell like speech, but
didn't seem to be a voice. Unless it was a giant's voice . . .

An interminable length of time later she came to the end
of the tunnel. The reek here was almost unbearable. Light
spilled down the tunnel from the gap at its end—a sickly sort
of light that flickered as though it was thrown by torches or
candles. And the booming sound *was* a voice. A huge voice
that had to belong to one of the giants. He was cursing the
Court for their inability to find one Jack—"ONE LITTLE
SHITHEAD OF A JACK." Underlying his roaring was a
constant chitter and rattle of other voices—bogans swearing,

hags hissing, gullywudes, spriggans and other creatures all
adding to the babble. Feeling as though her heart was in her
throat, Jacky crept forward.

The end of the tunnel was blocked with boulders. When
she dared her first peep over them, she realized that this wasn't
so much a bolthole as an airhole, for she was looking down
into an immense chamber. The floor was invisible, covered
with a moving carpet of bodies. The Unseelie Court swarmed
in that stone hall.

Jacky ducked quickly back. Lovely. Perfect. Not only were
there more of the creatures than she'd ever imagined waiting
for her down there, but unless she managed to grow wings,
she had no way to get down. She leaned despondently against
the wall of the tunnel. Who was she kidding? What could she
do down there anyway, except end up in someone's stewpot?

The constant babble of noise, with the roar of more than
one giant thundering overtop it as they argued with each other,
was almost more than she could bear. It wouldn't let her
think. The stench wouldn't let her breathe. Her helplessness
made her want to scream with frustration. Or cry. It all
seemed so useless.

Oh, she'd been filled with sharp criticism for the Seelie
faerie who wouldn't dare storm the Giants' Keep. Oh, yes. It
was easy to be brave and make brave noises then. But with
the Court gathered below her now . . . when she knew their
strengths, their sheer *numbers* . . . The voice of her panic
was starting up its GoJackyGoJackyGo chant inside her. Get
out of here while you can. NowNowNow.

She frowned at herself. Well, she'd go all right. But not
back up the tunnel. Not to safety. Not when Kate needed her
help down there. Not when the Laird's daughter was suffering
so.

She gathered up the ragged bits of her courage and peeped
over the boulders again, this time taking a good long look.
She saw the giants—five of them sitting along one wall, with
a sixth, that had to be the biggest living creature she'd ever
seen, sprawled on a throne roughly-carved from the face of
the rock behind him. That one had to be Gyre the Elder.

Fearful of being spotted, but determined to spy out what
she could, she studied the huge hall, looking for some trace
of Kate or the other Seelie Faerie that had come to Calabogie

with them, looking for Lorana, looking for . . . She saw the Horn then, hanging from the wall behind Gyre the Elder at a height that only a giant could reach. Even in the uncertain lighting she could make out the red dotting on it.

Rowans had red berries, she remembered, so that must be what Bhruic had meant about it being marked by the berries of her name. Except he'd also said it would be hidden. So what did it mean that it was just hanging there on the wall? Either Bhruic had his information wrong—and where would he have gotten it from anyway? she wondered with renewed suspicion—or there was a trick of some sort going on here.

She wished Kerevan was with her—that he'd stayed to help. He seemed up on all the faerie tricks, if you believed half of what he said. But if he was a trickster, well, he'd called her one too. *From one puck to another,* he'd said.

I need a trick of my own, she thought. I need to clear this place of the Host so that I can get my hands on the Horn. But she had nothing on her—and there was nothing in the tunnel that she could use. She studied the huge chamber once more, marking how, though it had been naturally formed, it bore the signs of toolwork as well. The throne, the stone benches along its walls, perhaps this very airhole, had been carved from what had originally been merely a naturally-formed cavern. Then she saw something she hadn't noticed before.

She'd been so busy looking down that she never thought to look about at her own height. There was a cleft running in the stone, at about the height of the top of the tunnel. Under it was a small ridge about five inches wide. She could just reach the cleft from the mouth of the tunnel—she was sure of it. That could take her around above and behind the giant's throne to where the Horn was—though how she'd hook it up into her hands from the precarious perch she'd be in, she didn't know. But the ridge also went to another opening about two thirds of the way around the hall. This one looked larger than the one she was hidden in. Perhaps it led down to the main floor. Or to wherever they kept their prisoners.

Jacky bit at her lip as she studied the cleft and the ridge below it. In some places the distance between the two would be a real stretch. She'd be in plain sight of anyone who chanced to look up. And it wasn't exactly going to be a stroll

in the park either. If she fell . . . But it was that, or give up
and go back the way she'd come.

GoBack! her panic told her. GoBackNowGoBack!

She shook her head. Below her, the giants' argument was
getting ugly. There were thundering roars of "SPIKE YOU!"
and "STEW YOU, ARSEBREATH!" and the Court itself
was jabbering away, louder than ever. Arguing. Taking sides.

It was now or never, Jacky told herself.

She climbed over the boulders and reached for the cleft.
The rock was firm at least—not crumbly as she'd feared. Taking a deep breath, she swung herself out, one foot still at the
mouth of the tunnel, the other scrabbling for purchase on the
ridge. There wasn't much room on it. But it would do. It
would have to do. Closing her mind to the babble of fear that
came bubbling up inside her, she swung completely out. Then
refusing to look down for all that she was sure that every eye
was on her, she began to inch her way along the ridge, making for the other opening she'd spied across the hall.

CHAPTER
21

The wooden beam that Kate was cutting free was the bottom horizontal one. When it fell, and if they could roll it away, they'd be able to squeeze out through the space that was left. And after that. . . . She closed her mind to what came after that. What she had to concentrate on at the moment was what she was doing now. She had already cut through half the ropes holding the beam in place, working her way slowly from right to left. The great wooden beam was beginning to sag.

"Just a few more," Arkan said. He was crouched beside her, eyes agleam. "And then we'll spike some bogans."

Kate shook her head. Half the time Arkan seemed ready to crawl into a hole and the other half he was ready to take on the world. He was certainly no slouch when it came to a fight—she hadn't forgotten the way he'd handled himself at the ambush—but she had to wonder at the seesaw aspect of his character.

"Here it goes," she said as her little penknife cut through the last bit of the rope she was working on.

She moved away as the beam tilted, trembled, then its unbalanced weight dropped it to the stone floor with a loud thunk. In their cell, the five prisoners held their breath. When no one came, Kate quickly began to saw through the last couple of ropes so that they could roll the log away from the

170

front of their cell. Thankfully, the floor sloped downward, away from then.

When she got to the last rope, the other four joined her at the front of the cell. As soon as the rope gave away, Arkan and Eilian kicked the beam. It hit the ground with a louder thunk and began to roll away from them.

"Let's go!" Kate cried.

She grabbed Moddy Gill and pushed her towards the opening, squeezing through after her. Arkan, Eilian and Finn were quick to follow. The beam rolled down the corridor, setting up a huge racket now. The sound, echoing from the walls and ceiling, rebounded, growing in volume. Bogans appeared down the hall, scrambling for cover as they saw the huge log rolling towards them. One wasn't quick enough and his shriek as the beam crushed him pierced their ears. On their feet now, the five of them ran after the beam.

"Where do they keep Lorana?" Eilian asked Moddy Gill, running at her side.

A bogan jumped out at them and Kate stabbed him with her little knife. She wasn't sure what she was expecting, but she certainly wasn't prepared for the bogan's reaction. It was though she'd run him through with a sword. He howled, tearing himself free, almost tugging the penknife from her hands. But then, instead of attacking her again, he merely clutched at his stomach and fell to the floor, moaning.

"She won't be in her cell just yet," Moddy Gill said. "They'll be bringing her in about now."

"Bringing her in from where?"

"Oh, they hang her out on the cliffs by day—curing her, you know?"

Eilian blanched. They reached Kate where she stood over the bogan. Collecting himself, Eilian tugged at Kate's arm.

"Well done," he said. "Now let's keep moving."

But they were too late. The corridor in front of them was suddenly filled with swarming creatures. Before anyone else could react, Kate ran forward, brandishing her little Swiss penknife, feeling like a fool. But the creatures directly threatened by its steel blade, tiny though it was, fell back in frantic haste to get away from it. Unfortunately, not all of the Host was so affected by iron. There were bogans and other crea-

tures who had become as much acclimatized to it as the Seelie faerie.

These pushed forward and when Kate stabbed at one of
them, he smashed the penknife from her grip with a curse
and then used the flat of his big hand to club her to the
ground. Gullywudes and spriggans, and a bogan or two, leapt
away from where the penknife skittered across the stone floor,
throwing up sparks. Then the whole crowd rushed forward to
attack.

In moments they were subdued once more and hauled back
to face Gyre the Elder. Their captors were none to gentle in
their treatment of the prisoners. They were bruised and bat-
tered, with Kate almost too dizzy to stand on her own, as
they were brought before the giant. His ugly face snarled
down at them, a special hatred in his eyes when he saw his
own daughter with her pig's head on her shoulders standing
there with them.

"WHERE'S YOUR JACK?" Gyre the Elder demanded of
them. "TELL ME, AND MAYBE I WON'T MAKE YOU
SUFFER LIKE SOME."

As he said that, the prisoners caught their first glimpse of
the Laird of Kinrowan's daughter. She was being brought
back from the cliff and taken to her cell for the night. Two
bogans supported her, dragging her roughly between them by
her wings. Her head lolled against her chest.

"GIVE ME YOUR JACK AND YOU'LL BE SPARED
THIS."

Kate could hardly focus her vision. All she saw hanging
between the two bogans was a fuzzy shape. But Eilian cried
out in anguish, while Finn hid his eyes. Arkan stared, then
looked away. Any hope he'd had was burned away at the sight
of Lorana's torment.

"THE JACK, YOU TURD-SUCKING BUGS!" Gyre the
Elder roared. "GIVE HER TO ME!"

Kate tried to face him, but everything just kept spinning
around her. The blow on her head had almost made her forget
where she was. This was just a nightmare and it didn't make
sense that anything could have a face as big as this thunder-
voiced monster did. She tried to speak, but the words stumbled in her throat and wouldn't come out.

"I'LL PULL YOUR LIMBS OFF, ONE BY ONE," the

giant swore, "UNTIL ONE OF YOU TELLS ME. I'LL POP
YOUR HEADS! I'LL CHEW YOU TO PIECES!"

He reached for Kate.

When Jacky reached the larger opening, she collapsed in
it and lay weakly there, unable to move. She had cramps in
her fingers and cramps in her calves and her neck muscles
were so knotted from tension that she didn't think they'd ever
loosen up again. It was long minutes later before she could
even roll over and peer down once again.

She was very close to Gyre the Elder and his throne now.
The floor of the cavern was a good forty foot drop from her
hiding place, but the head of the giant on his throne was no
more than ten feet or so down, and about five over. The Horn,
hanging there from its thong on the wall, was another fifteen
feet over.

I'll never reach it, she thought. And she had no tricks.

She slumped back against the wall of this new tunnel, too
tired to be curious about where it went. She tried to massage
her neck, but it didn't help. She noticed her gift from Bhruic
then and pulled the brooch free from her jacket, turning it
over in her hands. A tiny silver rowan staff, crossed by a sprig
of berries. Why couldn't it have been magic? A special kind
of magic something or other that would even work in a place
fouled by the Unseelie Court. But that, of course, would make
everything too easy, and things were never easy. Jacky had
discovered that a long time ago.

She heard a rumbling sound, above the cacophony of the
crowd below her. It sounded like something rolling down a
stone corridor. She looked out across the cavern as a quiet
fell across the giants and their Court. Now what was that?
And could she use it to some advantage? She was ready for
any sort of help. At this point she'd even welcome Bill Mur-
ray and his Ghostbusters. At least they'd make her laugh and
she needed a laugh right about now. It was that, or cry from
frustration.

But then she saw what the disturbance had been caused by
as a number of prisoners were dragged in front of Gyre the
Elder's throne. Her heart gave a surprised little jump at the
sight of Eilian, but that died quickly.

Oh, Kate, she thought. I never meant to get you into this. Why couldn't you just have stayed home? ·

She listened to Gyre the Elder rant, saw the bruises on Kate's face, saw the pitiable figure of the Laird of Kinrowan's daughter dragged into the cavern as well, saw that Eilian and the others were all going to die. When Gyre the Elder reached for Kate, something just snapped in Jacky.

She scrambled to her feet. Backing up a few paces, she ran forward and launched herself at the broad, ugly head of Gyre the Elder. The GoJackyGoJackyGo chant was roaring in her ears again, but this time it was fed by adrenaline, not panic. She landed with a jarring thump against the monster's skull and started to slide down the side of his head, gripping at his greasy hair with one hand to stop her descent while she stabbed at him with the heavy pin of her brooch.

"You want a Jack?" she screamed in his ears as she slid by it to his shoulder. "I'll give you a Jack!"

Gyre the Elder turned his face around and down towards her and she stabbed him in the eye. He roared and started to stand. One meaty hand flew to his wounded eye. Jacky tumbled from his shoulder. Her hand closed on the thong of the pendant the giant wore around his neck, but it snapped under her weight and she fell with it to his lap. But before she could regain her balance and get away, he was standing and she tumbled from his lap right into the crowd of bogans holding Kate and the others captive.

Gyre the Elder swung his head back, roaring from the pain in his eye, and cracked his head against the stone wall behind him. Stunned, he rose and staggered to one side, away from his throne. One huge leg kicked out, scattering bogans and the like in all directions. His younger brother rushed to help him, but he was too late. Gyre the Elder dropped like a felled oak, arms pinwheeling uselessly for balance.

When he landed, the cavern floor shook and rumbled. Directly above his head was the entrance of the airhole through which Jacky had entered. The largest of the boulders there tottered, then dropped from the ledge to crack the giant's head wide open. Blood fountained from the wound. His huge limbs kicked and jumped like a fish floundering in the bottom of a fisherman's boat. And then he lay still.

While all gazes were locked on the dying giant, Jacky rose

to her feet only to stare at the Horn that hung uselessly out
of reach. Any moment now, she knew, the creatures of the
Host were going to come to their senses and grab her. Could
she get to the Horn in time? Could she throw something at it
and hope to knock the Horn down and catch it before it shattered on the stone floor? Right. Why not ask if a bogan could
sit down and have a cup of tea with Kate's Auntie?

But adrenaline still rushed through her, firing her courage.
She picked up the nearest thing at hand—a twist of gold that
had once been a candlestick- -and meant to give a try at
knocking the Horn down.

"SMASH THEM!" Gyre the Younger roared, rising up
from beside his brother's corpse. "CRUSH THEM! SPIKE
THEM!"

A bogan rushed for Jacky, but Moddy Gill jumped in his
way and tangled up his feet so that he fell down, taking the
next few charging creatures down with him. Jacky drew back
her arm to throw the twisted candlestick, but then she saw
the box sitting at the foot of the dead giant's throne. The
rubble was thick there, broken bottles and trash, mixed with
more precious things like real jewels and gold and silver gob-
lets. And sitting in amongst it all was a delicate wooden box
with a berried tree carved onto its lid.

Oh, you sly bastard, Jacky thought.

A gullywude jumped onto her shoulder. More grabbed her
legs, trying to pull her down, but she dragged them with her
as she moved forward. She brought the candlestick down on
top of the box with a jarring blow and the wood shattered.
Oh, a horn hung there on the wall by the throne, in plain
sight for all to see, complete with its speckle of red for berries, and who'd think to look further? And who could get it
down but a giant? Anyone else trying would be caught so fast
it would make their head spin.

Well, my head's spinning now, Jacky thought, but it was
from success. Out of the ruin of the box she pulled a strange
twisting shape of a horn. The gullywudes were a swarm on
her, trying to drag her down. Gyre the Younger was looming
over her. The other four giants were wading through the
Court, knocking their folk everywhichway in their hurry to
get at her. But neither the gullywudes, nor the threat of the
giants and their Court, nor the fear of what using that Horn

might mean could stop her now. She dragged her arms up, gullywudes hanging from them, brought the mouthpiece of the Horn to her lips, and she blew it.

The sound of it was loud and fierce. At that first blast, the Court drew back from her—even the giants. She blew it again and again until its sound was all that filled the cavern—a wild, exulting sound that thrilled the blood in her veins, making it roar in her ears. She could feel its power fill her. The Hunt was coming. The Wild Hunt. And she was its mistress now.

She stepped away from the throne and Gyre the Younger moved to take it, sitting down to glare at her. The Court had cleared a great space around her. Her friends stood or lay around her. Kate and Eilian. Finn and Arkan. Lorana lay sprawled where her bogan guards had dropped her. There was a pig-headed woman there too—the one that had stopped the bogans from taking her as she'd lunged for the Horn.

Jacky brought the primitive instrument down from her lips and surveyed the Court. They could all hear it now—a distant sound like the rushing of wind, like the echoes of the Horn's blasts, like answering horns, winding out from dark cold places beyond the stars.

Of her friends, Eilian was the first to move. He tugged Kate and Moddy Gill, each by an arm, to stand behind Jacky. Finn and Arkan followed, Arkan carrying the frail limp shape of the Laird of Kinrowan's daughter. There were tears in his eyes as he pulled loose the nettle tunic and freed her from the Unseelie spell that had held her.

But Gyre the Younger, sitting on his dead brother's throne, he never moved. Nor did his Court. They knew enough to know that it was not who held the Horn but who blew it, and thereby summoned the riders, that ruled the Hunt. The blasting sound of that Horn had frozen them, sapping their strength, forbidding them to lift a hand against the Jack that the Seelie Court had sent against them.

And Jacky . . . the power of command boiled in her. What couldn't she do now, with this Horn in her possession? Then there was no more time to think.

The Hunt was come.

They didn't ride their Harleys here. They came on great horned steeds, horses with flanks that glittered like metal, but were scaled like fishscales. Stags' antlers lifted from the brows of the proud mounts. While the riders . . . They were cloaked in black, each one of them, all nine of them, come to the summoning. The leader stepped his mount closer, its hooves clipping sparks from the stone as it moved. The face that looked down at Jacky was grim, but not unhandsome. It was the eyes that made it alien—for there was no end to their depths. They studied her with disinterest, remotely. Obeying, but not caring who or what it was that summoned them.

"We have come," the leader said.

At his words, the cavern seemed to shiver. Jacky's friends and the Unseelie Court alike trembled, wishing they were anywhere but here. Only Jacky stood firm. With the Horn in her hand, nothing could stop her, no one could hurt her. That was what it promised her. But as she opened her mouth to speak, to command the Hunt, to send out the doom that would take down this Unseelie Court, once and forever, Kerevan's words came back to her, as though from a great distance, warning her.

From one puck to another . . .

I'm not a puck, she told that whispering memory, but she knew the words to be a lie. The Jacks were always pucks. They were the fools and the tricksters of Faerie, and knowing that, she knew that Kerevan's true name was Jack as well.

The Horn is too great a power. . . .

But that's just what we need to undo the evil of the Unseelie Court, she replied. Don't you see?

It corrupts any being that wields it. . . .

I'm not going to wield it. I'm only going to use it once— that's all. Just once.

But she knew that to be a lie as well. Why should she give up the power that the Horn offered her? Why let it fall into another's hands? It was better that she used it. Better that she chose who the Hunt chased, and who it didn't.

What would you command? the voice of memory forced her to ask herself. *That any who disagree with you be slain?*

I won't be like that. I'm fighting evil—I'm not evil myself.

It corrupts any being that wields it. . . .

Then what should I do? she demanded of that memory, but to that question it remained strangely silent.

The steeds of the Hunt began to shift as though sensing her indecision. Gyre the Younger stirred on his brother's throne, his hatred for her, for the death she'd brought his brother, for the pain and defeat she'd brought them all, was beginning to overpower his fear of the Hunt. Hadn't his own brother commanded the Hunt before? Wouldn't it sooner listen to him, who *knew* what he needed done, than to this trembling Jack who stood there, overawed by it all?

Jacky could feel the change in the room. The Horn whispered, telling her of the power that could be hers. The Wild Hunt demanded to know why it was summoned. Kerevan's voice, in her memory, told her she was doomed. Gyre the Younger made ready to take the Horn, as he'd already taken his brother's throne, and crush this Jack under his foot with a pleasure that would never be equalled again.

I don't know what to do, Jacky admitted to herself.

Use us, the eyes of the Wild Hunt demanded.

I am power, the Horn told her. *Yours to wield.*

She could use it and doom herself, or not use it and the power would go to Gyre the Younger and doom her anyway. There was no middle road, no road at all. But then she laughed. No road? Wrong! That was the lie! There was only one road she could take and she knew it now. She straightened, stooped shoulders losing their uncertainty. She met the gaze of the Wild Hunt's leader without flinching from its alien depths.

"Dismount," she said. "Come here to me."

On the throne, Gyre the Younger froze, uncertain once more. From a small creature, weighted down with fear and ignorance, she had gained stature once more.

Inside her, the Horn's voice exulted. *You will not regret the power I can give you,* it told her.

But Jacky only smiled. She watched the Huntsman dismount stiffly and approach her. When he was only a couple of paces away, Jacky reached out with the Horn.

"Take it," she said.

The alien depths changed. Confusion swam in the Huntsman's eyes. "Take it?" he asked slowly, not lifting a hand.

Jacky nodded. "Take it. It's used to command you, isn't it? Well, take it and command yourself."

Now the gaze measured her carefully. "And what is the bargain you offer?"

"No bargain. Please. Just take it."

The Huntsman nodded slowly. "Do you understand what you are doing?"

Jacky wet her lips. "Yes."

"Hill and Moon," the Hunstman whispered. "To think such a day could come." He took the Horn reverently from her.

"NO!" Gyre the Younger roared. "YOU MUSTN'T!"

"Oh, Jacky!" Kate cried. "What've you done?"

Consternation lay across all their faces, except for Eilian's. He smiled as understanding came to him.

"For years beyond count we have answered this Horn's call," the Huntsman said. "Men and faerie both have commanded us. They have had us slay and slay and slay again. They have had us spy for them. They have had us capture their foes, then made us watch them be tortured. But never was there one being that saw beyond the power the Horn offered to *our* need." The Huntsman bent his knee to Jacky. "Lady, I thank you for our freedom." Then he rose and, dropping the Horn to the stone floor of the cavern, he ground it to pieces underfoot.

A great wind stirred in the cavern. When they saw the Horn destroyed, the stasis that had bound the Unseelie Court finally fell away. But there was no place for them to flee now. At each entranceway stood one of the horned steeds of the Hunt, and on its back, a grim-faced Huntsman.

"Go from here," the leader of the Hunt said to Jacky. "Take your friends and go. There is a reckoning to be made between my brothers and those who rule this Keep—a reckoning that you should not be witness to."

Jacky nodded. "But . . . but you're really free now, aren't you?"

The Huntsman smiled. In his eyes, the alien depths wavered and for one moment Jacky saw a being of kindness look out from those eyes. Then the moment was past.

"We are truly free," the Huntsman said, "once this final task is done. And this task we do for ourselves. Go now, Jacky Rowan. You have our undying thanks. We will never forget this gift you have given us."

He touched her shoulder gently and steered her towards the entranceway. One by one her companions fell in step beside her. Kate took her hand.

"I'm so proud of you," she whispered, for she understood now what Jacky had done.

Arkan carried the frail body of the Laird's daughter. Eilian and Finn walked with Moddy Gill between them. When they reached the cavernous doors of the Keep's main entrance, the doors swung open to let them out. They went through, and the huge doors thundered closed behind them.

It was night outside, dark and mysterious, and air had never tasted so clean and fresh before.

"Now what do we do?" Kate said, thinking of the long way home and how they had only their legs to take them.

"Now," said a voice from the shadows, "I'll take you all home."

Jacky turned to see Kerevan leaning against a tree. "Did you know what was going to happen in there?" she demanded.

He shook his head. "Not a bit of it. You did what none of us had even considered, Jacky Rowan. Now I found this car in a ditch, and with a wally-stane—well, two or three really—I've got it working again. The ride will be more cramped than comfortable, but better than walking, I think."

"Judith!" Kate cried. "You rescued Judith!"

"The very vehicle," Kerevan replied.

"I thought you said your magics were all tricks and illusions," Jacky said as they all made their way down the mountainslope to where the car was waiting for them.

Kerevan glanced at her, then winked. "I lied," he said.

CHAPTER
22

They gathered in the room of the Gruagagh's Tower that over-looked Windsor Park—what faerie called Learg Green. The room had settled from its shifting shadows and ghostly fur-nishings into a warm kitchen with chairs for all. Bhruic had removed the last of the spell from Moddy Gill who proved to be a plain-featured, friendly woman who now sat in a corner of the room with Arkan, telling him how she thought he was rather brave. Arkan appeared entranced. Finn perched on a stool, while Jacky and Eilian sat with Kate in the window-seat. Kerevan leaned with studied ease against the door near the hall.

The Gruagagh looked different. He was no longer dressed in his black robes, but wore trousers and tunic of various shades of brown and green. And he was smiling. The only one missing of those who had escaped the Giants' Keep was the Laird's daughter and she was safe at her father's Court once more, with her father's faerie healers to look after her.

"I have something for you, Jacky," Bhruic said.

He handed her some official looking papers which proved to be the deed to a house. This house—the Gruagagh's Tower. There in black and white was her name, Jacqueline Elizabeth Rowan. The owner of a new home.

"I told you I didn't want anything," Jacky said.

"Someone must live in the Gruagagh's Tower and who better than the Court's own Jack?"

181

"Where are you going?" she asked.

"I have a bargain with Kerevan to fulfill," he replied.

Kerevan grinned at Jacky when she turned to him and gave her a mocking, but friendly tug of the forelock. "And yes," he said, "I'm a Jack, too, though my Jack days are gone now. Jack Gooseberry was the name then, and wasn't I the wild one?"

"Too wild," Bhruic said wryly.

"I'd rather know why," Jacky said.

Bhruic sighed. "Why what?"

"Why couldn't you just have told us everything? Why were you so unfriendly? Why didn't you help more?"

Bhruic looked uncomfortable. He glanced at Kerevan, but there was no help there. The others in that room, except for Moddy Gill, were all giving him their full attention, for they too wanted the answer to those questions. Bhruic sighed again and pulled a chair closer to the windowseat.

"I didn't trust you," he said. "It was too convenient—a Jack out of nowhere, willing to help, Kate Crackernuts at her side. I thought you were one more attempt by the Host to pry me from my Tower. They knew my weakness better than my own Laird's folk ever did."

"Always sticking your nose in where it didn't have to go," Kerevan said.

"Always wanting to help those in trouble," Bhruic corrected him.

Kerevan shrugged. "Different ways of saying the same thing—that's all."

"I wanted to believe in you, Jacky Rowan," Bhruic went on. "Truly I did. But there was too much at stake. If it had been just myself, I would have taken the chance. But there was all of Kinrowan to think of as well."

"So now you're going and leaving me with"—she held up the deed to the Tower—"with this."

Bhruic nodded.

"But Samhaine night's still coming—and Kinrowan needs its Gruagagh."

"The Laird's daughter will be recovered enough by then, and we don't have the Unseelie Court to worry about—at least not this year. They'll grow strong again, they always do, but it will take time."

"But there's still got to be a gruagagh . . ."

"I thought a Jack such as you would be more than enough to take my place," Bhruic said.

"But *I* don't have any magics."

"Well, now," Kerevan said. "You've at least nine wally-stanes, and if you're sparing with them, and use your noggin a bit, you should do fine."

"But . . ."

"Oh, just think," Kate said. "Your own house. I think that's wonderful."

"But it's so big," Jacky protested half-heartedly.

She caught a smile pass between Bhruic and Kerevan and knew what they were thinking: She wanted to live here. She wanted to be Kinrowan's Jack. She didn't ever want to not know the magic of Faerie. They were right.

"If it's too big for you," Kate said, "then I'll move in with you. I'm not too proud to invite myself."

"So's it going to be a commune already?" Jacky asked. Her gaze flitted from Finn to Arkan.

"Not me," Finn said. "I've already got a snug little place just down the way from here, but I'll be dropping by for a hot cuppa from time to time. And there's always that comfortable perch in your tree between the Tower's garden and Learg Green—a fine place for a hob. You'll see me there often enough."

"I'm thinking of getting myself a wagon and pony," Arkan said, "and travelling some again. It's been years since I've seen the old haunts and Moddy here could use a new view or two."

It wasn't hard to see that they were already an item, Jacky thought. And speaking of items . . . shyer now, her gaze moved to Eilian. She was still attracted to the Lairdling, but wasn't sure how much of that was just her rebounding from Will and latching onto the first available—and gorgeous, she added to herself, let's admit it—fellow that came along.

Eilian smiled and lifted the hair at the back of his neck where the braids his Billy Blind had plaited hung. "I've one left," he said. "I wouldn't want to bring more trouble to you—I don't doubt you've seen enough to last a lifetime. But if there's room, I'd like to stay, at least till you're settled in."

"You see?" Bhruic said. "It's all settled."

"How come everybody settles things for me, but me?" Jacky wanted to know.

Bhruic smiled, but it was a serious smile. "I think that you settled everything yourself, Jacky Rowan, in a way that no other could, or perhaps even would have. You're the best Jack Faerie's known since, oh—"

"Me," Kerevan said without any pretense at modesty.

Jacky rolled her eyes. "Does this mean I have to learn to play the fiddle now?"

Kerevan shrugged. "There's worse fates."

"But not many," Bhruic added. "It's when you're learning the fiddle that you find out who your real friends are. It's no wonder they call it the devil's own instrument."

It was almost morning before those who were leaving actually took their leave. Arkan and Moddy Gill had slipped away rather quickly and Finn was asleep in one corner, with Kate nodding in another, when the Gruagagh, Kerevan, Eilian and Jacky went out into the park.

"I'm sorry it was so hard for you, Jacky," Bhruic said. "I'm sorry there was too much to risk that I couldn't trust your freely offered help. And as for that silence the last time you stayed in my Tower—you've Kerevan here to blame for that. It was part of my bargain for your safety that I not see you, or speak to you of our bargain."

"I know," Jacky said. "I just wish you weren't going away without my ever getting to know you. Why *do* you have to go now anyway? There's no more danger."

"But that's just it. I never wanted the mantle of a gruagagh. I was a poet first and a harper, Jacky." He nudged Kerevan. "This lug here was my master in those trades. Now that I know Kinrowan's safe, I can go back to being what I want to be."

"But what about me? What if I don't want to be Kinrowan's protector?"

"Don't you?"

That smile was back on the Gruagagh's lips again. Jacky thought about it, about Faerie and how her life had been before she fell into it. She shook her head. "If that's what it takes to live in Faerie, then I'll do it."

"You could live in Faerie without it."

"Yes . . . but then I'd just be wasting my time again. Now at least I'll have something meaningful to do."

"Just so."

"Except I don't know what it is that I *am* supposed to do."

"There's a hidden room on the third floor that will never be hidden from you, now that you are the Tower's mistress. The answer to your questions lie in it—it's not so hard. Not for a clever Jack like you."

"Yes, but . . ."

Bhruic smiled. "Farewell, Jacky Rowan, and to you, Eilian. Take good care of each other."

"The devil's own instrument!" Kerevan muttered, and then there was a rush of wind in the air, a taste of magic, and two swans, one white and one black, were rising on their wings into the wind. They circled once, twice, three times, dipping their wings, then they were gone, down the long grey October skies.

Jacky sighed and turned to Eilian. "Did you want to go with them?" she asked.

He shook his head.

"I did. Just a little. Just to be able to fly . . ." Her voice trailed off dreamily.

"I like it here just fine," Eilian said.

"Better than Dunlogan?"

"Much better than Dunlogan."

"Even though there aren't any swangirls here?"

"I never cared for swangirls. I always had my eyes set on a Jack—if I could ever find myself one."

"Even one with corn stubble hair?"

"Especially one with corn stubble hair."

"I can't make promises," Jacky said. "You're getting me on the rebound."

"I know."

They looked at each other for a long moment, then Jacky reached for his hand, captured it, and led him back to the Gruagagh's Tower. No, she amended. It's the Jack's Tower now.

"The trouble with Jacks," she said, "is once you've got one, they're often more trouble than they're worth."

Eilian stopped her on the back steps of the Tower and tilted her head up so that she was looking into his eyes. "So long as it's the right sort of trouble," he said.

He kissed her before she could think of a suitably puckish sort of a reply.

278